Love In Texas

"Finding Love"
Romance series
Book One

Written by
Kathy Uherhewar

ISBN: 9798539738303

Publication Date August 5, 2021
2nd Edition

Table of Contents

Epilogue
Chapter 1
Chapter 2
Chapter 3
Chapter 4
Chapter 5
Chapter 6
Chapter 7
Chapter 8
Chapter 9
Chapter 10
Chapter 11
Chapter 12
Chapter 13
Chapter 14
Chapter 15
Chapter 16
Chapter 17
Chapter 18
Chapter 19
Chapter 20
Chapter 21
Chapter 22
Chapter 23
Chapter 24
Chapter 25
Prologue
The Dream

Copyright 2021
Kathy Uherhewar
All Rights Reserved

This Book is dedicated to the only person who has ever believed in me, laughed with me, had my back, and loved me unconditionally. Her faith in me has always been my true saving grace. My number one cuz,
Jane Parrish Latham

My Book is a work of fiction. Names, businesses, places, and events are all figments of my imagination based on real happenings in my life twisted into fiction. Any resemblances to anything or anyone are just a coincidence.

Prologue

Her Story

As she sat by the pool, her sweet, iced tea forgotten she relived the arguments and the terrible words spoken. Her children knew how her life had been. Why could they not understand. She needed a change. A new life. A life far away from memories and people always stopping her in Walmart expressing their sorrow.

As her eyes fluttered, as she thought back to her previous life…….

Her job had ended and there was not a chance of finding a job in her small town. It had been almost three years since her abusive husband had passed away. After Twenty-three years of marriage, two children, four grandchildren, and years of mental abuse he had died of a massive heart attack. He went quickly. He just walked out the door to his truck and fell to the ground. By the time his friend Ronald Davidson pulled up to find him, he had been dead for twenty minutes. She did not find him.

Her daily routine had always been the same. As soon as he walked out the door, she did not look for him again until he came back in. It was the only time she felt peace. She would clean her house prep for dinner and supper. Then stowaway in her sewing room until time to make dinner. That is when Greggory, her husband came back. Always with a friend or two. She would serve them dinner, then head back to her sewing room until they left. It was the rule. She was not allowed to mingle and chat with his friends. He took that as flirting and would berate her in front of them, and later would accuse her of sleeping around with them. His friends were never at fault. It was always her and only her.

In the beginning he was charming and wonderful. He treated her like a queen. She had just graduated college and was working for a small-town lawyer as an assistant. She was twenty, her boss in his sixties and happily married. She had started dating Greggory six months before she graduated. He was the son of her father's best friend.

One day she was asked to work late. Greggory did not believe her. When he picked her up that evening, she noticed he was quieter than usual. As tired as she was, she did not pay much attention to it until he began driving erratically. He started accusing her of sleeping with her boss. She cried and begged him to believe her. He drove down a road near the river.

He stopped in a secluded area and yanked her from the truck. He whispered in her ear that if she was going to sleep with every man in town he might as well get his share. After all, she was his girl.

She was terrified of him. He had never acted this way before. She screamed for him to take her home, but he just kept pulling at her clothes. As he raped her, she just went limp and let him have his way. It was her first time. She had never even seen a naked man before. It was painful and he hurt her over and over. When he was finished, and he realized she had been a virgin he started crying, begging her to forgive him. She was too scared to do anything but go along with him. He held her and kissed her tears away. She cringed inside. All she wanted was to go home. Once he was all cried out, he drove her home.

She ran inside. Locking her door, she ran to her bathroom where she threw up over and over. When she had dry heaved her last, she threw her clothes she was wearing in the trash. She took a shower until the water turned ice cold. She crawled into bed and stayed for the rest of the weekend. She did not answer her phone, or the door. She did not ever want to see him again.

On Monday, he showed up at her job begging her to talk to him. She told him to leave her alone, and never speak to her again. Day after day he waited as she left work. He would bring flowers and candy, food, and jewelry. She would walk to her car, ignoring him. He would follow her home. She would run into her house and lock the door.

This went on for a month then one day it suddenly stopped. He was not out there. He did not follow her home; he did not call or bang on her door.

A week went by with nothing from him. She was almost afraid to be happy about it. Could it be true? Was he finally going to leave her alone? Then the paranoia set in. She was a nervous wreck. Always looking behind her. She became sick. Worried to death that it would all start up again at any moment.

Every morning was the same. She would wake up and be sick. The thought of food, making her nauseous. She lost weight.

Her job was suffering. One day her boss told her to go to the doctor and take a week off. She did but the results of her blood work left her cold.

She was pregnant!

It did not take long for word to spread in her small town. A week later she went back to work only to discover She had been replaced. Her boss called her into his office. He told her he was deeply sorry, but his wife was not comfortable with someone like her, working in his office. So that was it. She was jobless, labeled, and pregnant!

As the days went by, she thought about moving away. Her family would not hear of that. Her dad insisted she find the father and get married. When she told her parents who the father was, they were so excited and happy. Her dad called Gregory and congratulated him. He told him they could go to the courthouse and make the child legal. And that is how she wound up married to the man who raped her.

Her life was good for the first few years. He pampered her during her pregnancy and doted on her and their son when he was born. It was not long before she was pregnant again. Almost a year after her son Benjamin was born, she gave birth to a beautiful baby girl. She named her Allison.

Gregory was over the moon. He loved and adored his children, spoiling them with everything they wanted. As the years slipped by and the children started getting older the abuse started again. Never in public. Never in front of the children.

Her life became the same day over and over. Cook, clean, take care of him and the children. He always found fault in everything she did. Food was not cooked correctly; house was not clean enough. She Disciplined the children to much. And then, the accusation started. She was flirting with every man or sleeping with them.

Year after year her life became the same. She gained weight. She never wore nice clothes or makeup. She never got her hair fixed. She made her own clothes. Housedresses and ponytails became her way of life. If she was gone too long shopping she was cheating. If she spoke to any man, she was cheating. She never told anyone about her life except to her best friend from college.

Her best friend lived a few states away with her family. They never saw each other anymore, but they talked on the phone every week. They sent letters and pictures thru the mail. Missy, short for Melissa became her only source of happiness. She lived life thru her best friends' experiences. Missy would beg her to leave him. But she would not leave her children and could not take them away from him.

She lived for Someday.

Someday, they would be grown, and she could leave and never look back. Someday came when two years after her husband died, she found herself jobless with ten years left on a mortgage.

One of the first things she bought after Greggory died was a computer. She was not allowed to have one before. Every day she searched for jobs. She placed her resume on several online job sites. Six months after she lost her job, she received an email about a job interview. She replied, thinking it was in a nearby city and she could easily commute.

The day the phone interview happened, she discovered the job was in Texas, San Antonio, to be exact. It sounded too good to be true. It was with a swanky up and coming law firm. They were looking for employees that could learn their innovative way of thinking. The pay was excellent with many perks. They offered to fly her out to San Antonio for a personal interview. Before she had time to think about it, she said yes, she would go to the interview.

A week later she found herself twelve-hundred miles from home in a strange and beautiful city. She was booked into a nice downtown hotel. She fell in love with San Antonio Immediately.

It was like nowhere she had ever been before. She was offered the job, and she gladly accepted.

She went back home and sold her home to her son. And after weeks of arguments and tons of tears. she left Alabama. As she was driving out of town one of her favorite songs was playing on the radio.

I sold what I could packed what I couldn't. Stop to fill up on my way out of town……

Chapter One

The Present

She could not believe it. It was almost Thanksgiving and here she was in a sundress sitting out by the pool. Back home, the snow had already hit the five-inch mark. Her family was preparing for the holidays and here she was relaxing out in the sun. As her thoughts went back to home and family, she closed her eyes, her book already forgotten.

*The phone call with her daughter the previous day almost had the tears ready to fall again. Why could they not understand? She had only been in Texas for six months. She would not be eligible for vacation for twelve more months. It was in her contract; eighteen months of excellent job performance and she would be eligible for three weeks paid vacation. She needed that word **paid**. That meant she could afford to fly home, rent a car, and spend three weeks spoiling her grandchildren. Paid meant it would not affect her budget.*

She loved her job as an assistant to a high-ranking lawyer. Her college degree and work experience years ago, had not been for nothing. The last two years before she moved to Texas had also helped as she had been able to work with a small-town lawyer, but he had retired. And she was soon to be unemployed. Her boss had sold his business to a corporation in nearby Guntersville. She was given a year severance pay. Her home was almost paid for. The land and house were worth twice what her husband had paid for it twenty years before. But the children had been born and raised there and she did not have the heart to sell it. However, she would soon be out of money, and she had a year to find a job.

My cell phone was ringing, bringing me back from my memories. I looked at the phone and noticed it was my friend Missy, so I answered.

"Hey girl, what's up",

Missy laughed and said, "not much, are you going home for the holidays?"

"No, I can't go this year, but I will definitely be going next year, when are y'all coming out to visit?"

"Well, Charlie and I are thinking of coming up after New Year's. Does this work for you?"

"Sure does, you know you're welcome anytime."

"Are the kids giving you a hard time still?".

"Yes. I told them road runs both ways, but they think I left I should return."

Laughing she says, "Figured as much. They will never understand the years of abuse you suffered.

"No, they won't, because they never actually saw it.

"So, what are you doing today?"

"Laying out by the pool."

"Seriously, it's warm enough to swim?"

"The water is cold, but the sun is warm and feels so good." I could detect the envy in her voice as she said, "must be Nice."

I laughed and said, "Uh huh extremely nice. Almost as nice as this strikingly handsome man I am watching. He is getting in the hot tub."

Yelling and laughing she tells me, "Snap a pic, send it to me".

Knowing I was invading his privacy, I still could not resist snapping a few pics with my phone. As I sent them to her. I felt like a stalker. But good-looking guys were hard to find at my age, and this one was a looker.

Short dark hair with just enough gray at the edges to give him that distinguished look. Not tall, but not short. He looked to be about 5'7. He had a nice athletic body. His chest and abs were ripped. He looked to be the type who ran, or maybe played tennis or racquetball. I guessed him to be around the mid 50's. Today was not the first time I had seen him. I had saw him a couple of times coming and going in the parking lot. He was always dressed in military attire, being this was San Antonio, Military City, I deduced he was indeed military.

Suddenly I hear, "Hey hey hey are you still there?"

This brought me back to the present and fanning myself with my hand I answered. "Yes, I'm still here.

Giggling Missy said, "I thought maybe the hunk caught you snapping pictures and had you thrown out of the pool area."

"Nope he hasn't even looked my way. And why would he I'm not his type."

"What do you mean not his type?"

"You know, young, long legged and blonde. Men always want beautiful young trophy women on their arms, not an almost forty-seven-year-old grandmother with a weight problem."

Laughing Missy says, "girl, stop. You don't even look thirty-five much less almost forty-seven. And you lost a lot of weight after Gregory died. You're a looker, not an elderly grandmother."

"I am a flabby woman and yes, I know I'm insecure about my looks. Don't be so shocked. You Know I am not looking for a man anytime soon. I am doing the me right now. I don't think I even know how to behave with a man."

Exasperated Missy says, "my friend you spent many years being told you were someone that I know you are not. We have had this conversation before, over and over. Gregory was wrong to treat you that way. Not all men are like him. I got a good one and I'm sure when you least expect it you will find that perfect someone who will adore you and treat you like the queen, I know you are."

Laughing I said, "I know, I know, I know I need to get therapy I suppose."

Still Laughing she said, "I'm the only therapist you need. And I think you need to hang up and go get in that hot tub."

Giggling I said. "Yeah, that's not happening. I am not even wearing a bathing suit. But I do need to run I have some laundry to do and things to get ready before work tomorrow. I love you, talk soon. Hug your hubby for me."

After we hung up, I gathered my water down tea glass, my kindle and my cell phone and got up to leave the pool area. This meant walking past the area where the hottie in the hot tub was located.

I walked along the pool hoping I did not stumble along the way. Just as I walked past the hot tub, the hot cutie was getting out. At that moment he splashed water on the deck. As careful as I was trying to be, I still slipped on the slick deck. Losing my balance and flinging my arms I fell right into his strong muscled arms. He caught me as my tea glass, kindle, and phone went flying.

"Whoa, there pretty lady. "

I turned my head and stared into the most beautiful brown eyes and the sexiest smile I had ever seen.

"Oh," was all I could say.

We stood there gazing into each other eyes. It seemed like time had stood still, but it was just a fleet second. He stepped away from the edge of the hot tub an held my arm and I stepped to a dry area.

He stooped to retrieve my Kindle and cell phone. Luckily, my tea glass was plastic. The watered-down tea has spilled on the deck. As I watched the tea running a stream along the deck, I bent down to pick up my glass. "Well," I said, "I guess I'd better go get a mop and clean this mess up".

He handed me my kindle and phone and spoke. " It was my fault. I'll clean it up."

I thanked him and quickly walked away. I was so embarrassed. All I could think about was getting back to my apartment. I hurried into the lobby. Normally I take the stairs, but my legs were like jelly so I decided the elevator would be better. I punched *up* on the elevator buttons. The doors opened and I rushed in and hit my floor number and the *close door* buttons quickly,

As I unlocked the door to my apartment, I heard steps in the stairwell. I shut my door and locked it. I ran into the bathroom and saw my face in the mirror.

A wild-eyed woman stared back at me. I splashed water on my face and told that woman to calm the Hell down. That is when the woman in the mirror turned into gorgeous brown eyes and a beautiful smile.

Shaking my head to clear the illusion away I gathered up my laundry basket. After all, it was laundry night.

Chapter Two

His Story

Who was that gorgeous woman? Why have I not seen her around before. I did not make a great first impression by splashing water on the deck, but if it meant she would fall into my arms again, I would repeat it over and often. Wonder where she was from. The southern twang in her voice was different. Not Texas more a deep south Twang. I would have to ask around about her, starting with Gary, the security guard. His job was to know all the tenants. I would definitely pick his brain at our next Poker Night.

I had not had the time or patience to date lately. The pickings were slim to none. The younger women only wanted to date men with deep pockets and who liked to party. I did not have deep pockets, but I was far from starving. My party days had ended in my late twenties.

Having never married before, I had made the Air Force My lady, I spent years traveling all over the world being stationed in many different countries.

Getting married and having kids was something I could not do. I watched too many of my fellow officers' lives turned upside down from having wives and children. Some wives chose to be with their husbands, and that meant, uprooting their children time after time at each new duty station. Others chose to stay in one place, raising the children all alone.

It was a life I had never wanted. I was not too old to start a family, but I was not interested in the young ladies, and the ladies I was interested in, were almost past that prime time in life to have children.

I would be fifty-five in May. Thirty-five years in the Air Force. I had joined right out of college, working my way up the ranks to Lieutenant Colonel. Now I shuffled papers all day with procurement work. Occasionally traveling with or for the Colonel to different Military Bases. I did not have any family left.

My parents had passed away years ago and my only brother who was nineteen years older than me had died in Vietnam. I was what was called back then a change of life baby. My parents were in their late forties when I was born.

Since joining the Military, I had lived everywhere. Originally from Arizona. I had done my basic training in San Antonio. I was getting nearer to retirement, so I took a cushy office job at Lackland in San Antonio.

I was perfectly happy in my life. Working all week. Sometimes traveling. I had a bowling night. A Poker Night. And the dreaded laundry night. The rest of my time I spent sleeping and catching up on TV shows.

I enjoyed cooking my own meals but, more often after working late hours I would eat out. Some weekends I went out to a friend's ranch, and we would go camping or fishing or horseback riding. Occasionally, a group of us would hit the Kickapoo casino down in Eagle Pass. We enjoyed this time. But the best times were spent flying out to Vegas on three-day weekends.

I spent my summer vacations down in South Texas on Padre Island. I had a small cottage I had invested in on the beach. I used it often but when I was not, I had it listed with a local real estate company as an Air-BNB. This helped to pay the taxes and upkeep with a little left to grow the savings account.

I thought my life was pretty much perfect. Until blue green eyes and the most kissable lips I had not seen in a long while slipped into my arms. At first, I thought maybe she did not speak English as the only words out of her mouth were "oh".

A pink tinged blush on her face made her look so darn cute. But as she started walking away talking about getting a mop, I knew I had to hear that twang again.

She looked to be in her late thirty's early forties. I did look at her ring finger and did not see a ring. I could not tell if she was taken, but I was going to find out.

She was not tall about five foot one or two. She had soft feminine curves. A body that was not fat nor skinny. Her long brown hair was silky and fell halfway down her back. She had tiny feet and perfect toes with the nails painted fire engine red. She had an unforgettable face, gorgeous eyes, long eyelashes, and full kissable lips.

As I finished cleaning up her spilled drink, I found myself thinking that this was someone I could really see myself with. I had noticed her when I first went out to the pool. She was on the far end talking on her phone. Every now and then I could hear her laugh. I thought whoever she was talking to must have been a comedian. I had never heard someone laugh so much in a conversation. Her laugh was intoxicating.

I could not hear her words, but I did notice her looking my way a time or two. When she got up to leave, I could tell she was taking careful steps like she was afraid of falling in the pool.

As she got closer, I deliberately splashed the water as I got out of the hot tub hoping to have a chance to speak if only to say sorry did not mean to splash. The last thing I ever dreamed of was her slipping and falling. If I had not caught her, she would have fell sideways into the hot tub. Possibly hitting her head or breaking a bone. Thankfully, my reflexes were quick enough to catch her.

I knew it embarrassed her, so I did not bother with more conversation. I just took the blame. I said I would clean the spilled drink up.

She left in a rush. I ran after her once my senses came back, but she had taken the elevator. I took the steps two at a time. By the time I heard the elevator doors open she had already gone into her apartment.

I heard the door shut at apartment 4201. I was in 3201. Right below her. Why had I not ever seen her before. You would think I would have noticed someone that beautiful living in the same apartment building as me. I should have at least saw her in and out of the parking lot.

Maybe she had just moved in. Maybe she had a boyfriend or partner or husband. I knew one thing. I was most definitely going to find out. Putting speaking to Gary at the top of my list.

A few hours later I gathered my laundry basket and headed down to the laundry room. After all this was laundry night.

Chapter Three

Maggie

Doing laundry was always a three-hour job. I only did laundry every other Sunday night. It usually took two weeks to have enough for a load to wash. My work clothes were taken to the dry cleaners, but my personal garments, towels and sheets were washed by me.

The laundry room had six sets of machines. A large folding table and a cute little sitting area with a couch and a couple of comfy chairs. There was a soft drink and a snack machine along one wall, as well as a change maker.

The luxury apartments were genuinely nice but did not have laundry accommodations inside the apartments. I always love doing laundry, but mostly I missed hanging my sheets and towels outside on a clothesline. I missed the fresh smell the sunshine put into them. I notice not many homes in San Antonio had clotheslines. That was a real shocker for me because back home everyone had clothesline.

The laundry room rule was to not use all the machines at one time. You could only use two at most. So, my six loads every two weeks took a couple of hours. I would bring two loads down and sit in the sitting area and read while they washed. Then I would go back to my apartment to get two more loads. I would wash rinse dry fold. Take those two loads back to the apartment, get the next two loads and do it all over again.

Using the stairs each time convinced me I was getting great exercise, like using a stair master or a treadmill.

The apartment complex had a great workout room, but I felt too embarrassed to use them. I tried staying away from places that were usually full of people.

I had just placed my last load in the dryer and was folding my towels when I suddenly realized I was not alone. Looking behind me, I saw Mr. Brown Eyes. As he walked towards the washing machine, he smiled that beautiful smile and spoke.

"So, we meet again."

I laughed and said, "seems that way."

He placed his clothes in the washer and sat down in one of the chairs, pulling his phone out of his pocket. I did not know whether to fold slower or hurry and fold quickly so I could go sit back down. I am not a take the first initiative type woman. On my job I was very much a go getter, but in my private life I was extremely shy and self-conscious.

I finished folding, then checked the time on my sheets. Thankfully, my first two loads had been my personal items and had already been taken back up to my apartment. I walked over to my chair and sat down. He put his phone away and spoke.

"I want to apologize again for splashing water on the deck. I really did not intend for you to slip and fall. It could have been a serious injury if you had fallen into the hot tub."

I smiled. "Well good thing you caught me when you did. I would hate for you to feel guilty over causing me serious injury."

He laughed. "This is true. I would have felt terrible, but I have no regrets about holding you in my arms."

Once again, I could not think of anything to say but "oh."

He stood up and as he walked toward the soda machine said,

"Can I buy you a soda?"

I knew he knew I was struggling to find words by the way my face turned a beet red. He was being a gentleman, offering to buy drinks and leave me to collect myself.

As he walked toward the soda machine, I said. "Yes, a Pepsi please,"

He walked back over with my Pepsi and his root beer. Smiling up at him, I said, "thank you."

He began the conversation by asking me, "how long have you lived in these apartments?"

"Six months in Texas and the apartment. How long have you lived here or are you a San Antonio native?"

"I have been in San Antonio about five years this time and in the apartment about the same amount,"

"What do you do for a living if I may ask."

"You may, I shuffle papers around."

I laughed. "Must be nice. Does that pay well?"

Smiling, he responded "well enough. And what do you for a living? If I may also ask?"

"Well, I shuffle papers too, I'm an executive assistant to a new up-and-coming law firm here in San Antonio and yes, it pays well."

He just sat there smiling that beautiful smile, knowing how nervous it made me. When my dryer and his washer both buzzed at the same time, we both got up and I bumped right into him. He caught my arms, my lips just inches from his and he said.

"We have to stop meeting this way."

I did not realize I was holding my breath until he released my arm and moved to his washing machine.

I walked over and retrieved my sheets from the dryer. Part of me wanted to just throw them in the basket and leave, but my OCD insisted that I fold the sheets properly.

I was struggling with the folding when he suddenly grabs two ends and said, "let me help you."

I shrugged my shoulders and said, "OK thanks."

We folded my two sets of sheets and placed them in the basket. I picked up the basket, turned to him saying,

"It was a pleasure to meet you again and thank you again for the soda."

I turned and walked out to the stairwell. He caught up with me and said,

"Let me carry that for you".

I wanted to say I got it, but that smile had me saying.

"OK thanks again"

As we walked up the four flights of stairs, he talked about the apartments and that side of town. He asked if I had learned to drive with the two loops around the city. I told him I was still very much confused about driving and was glad I had GPS. I told him that I had already spent several weekends just driving the loops to see the outer and inner areas of San Antonio, and I had figured it out already. If I was ever lost driving in San Antonio, I just had to find my way to one of those two loops and drive. I would eventually find my side of town. He laughed and said that was smart thinking.

When we reached my door, I push the buttons to unlock my lock and opened the door. He sat the basket just inside the door. He turned to walk away, then suddenly stopped, turned back and said.

"By the way, I didn't catch your name."

I laughed. "I never threw it at you. But it is Maggie. and yours is?"

With a proud flourish he half bowed, "Lieutenant Colonel Colin Douglas, at your service mam.

"Well, it's been a pleasure to meet you, Lieutenant Colonel Colin Douglas."

As an afterthought he smiled and said, "Would you like to grab coffee or dinner sometime?"

Smiling I answered "Yes, that would be nice,"

I walked into my apartment, picked up the basket and carried it to my bedroom closet. After putting all the items away. I sat down on my bed as I pulled my phone from my pocket. I called Missy. When she answered, I just blurted out the whole thing from the pool to the laundry room to outside my door. Fifteen minutes later, I stopped to catch my breath.

"He even asked me for coffee or dinner sometime. Sometime!! Not a particular time, just sometime."

Laughing out loud she then whispered, "wow. Way to go, girl. I bet sometimes happens before next weekend."

We spent the next two hours talking about everything I needed to hear to give me the confidence I needed to wait until sometime.

Chapter Four

Thanksgiving Eve

Maggie

It was the day before Thanksgiving. The office was closing early, and I was busy shutting my computer down. I was glad to be getting off work early. The office would not open again until Monday. I had four and a half days off.

I had not seen Brown eyes for over two weeks. But then why would I? Our last conversation was a tentative sometime, but it did not stop me from thinking about him. I was always looking for him in the parking lot.

I had not gone back out to the pool since that day. I did not want it to appear like I was looking for him.

As I took the elevator to the parking garage, I mentally made a shopping list. I was not going to cook a Thanksgiving dinner this year. It would be a first for me in twenty-six years, but there was not anyone to cook for an I did not feel in the mood to cook food for one.

At the local grocery I added a frozen Turkey dinner to my cart. I did not much care for frozen dinners, but this one time would not hurt. After thirty minutes in the store, I was finally on my way home.

A sadness suddenly enveloped me.

By now back home my house would be fully decorated for Christmas. A fresh cut tree would be standing in the alcove waiting for Thanksgiving night to be decorated by the children. My house would have the smells of the holiday waffling around me, My Apple pies, Pumpkin Pies and Pecan pies would all be cooling on a shelf. My cakes beautifully decorated proudly displayed in tier plates on my buffet. A Turkey would be prepped and waiting in the refrigerator. My cornbread dressing already prepared in the fridge waiting to be placed in the oven. I always pre prepared a lot of the menu the day before so I would have more time to spend with my family on Thanksgiving Day, without rushing to fix food.

But this year would be my first alone. There would be no fresh baked pie smell. No fresh cut tree smell. No Thanksgiving dinner to prepare. Sadness took over and the tears started to fall. I love my new life. My job and my cute apartment, but I so dearly missed my home and my children and grandchildren.

They were growing up so fast. Little Benji and Logan were almost three. Sophia and Olivia had just turned one. Both girls were walking now. I had missed out on that. I found time several times a week to FaceTime with the four children. The boy's always telling me the cutest new thing they were doing.

Benji was into horses and always talked nonstop about his new pony my son Benjamin had gotten him the previous summer. Benji was learning to barrel race. His mother, my daughter in law Brittney, had barrel raced all her life. Teaching her children was a joy. She had given up the barrel racing rodeo days when she married my son. She devoted her life to being a wife and mother.

My daughter's son Logan was the same age as Benji. Both boys born a week apart. Logan was into games. He would talk nonstop about the latest video game he and my son in law Joshua were into. I loved to watch his face as he bragged about beating his dad. I of course knew Joshua allowed that to happen. He was a wonderful father and husband to my daughter Allison. Joshua was an EMT, Allison was an RN.

My two granddaughters were born hours apart. Sophia, Benjamin's daughter was born a few minutes before midnight and Olivia, Allison's daughter was born at Four AM. So, both girls had different birth dates. They were beautiful girls and loved to jabber to grandma on FaceTime.

My son Benjamin had bought my farm from me before I left Alabama. I paid the mortgage off and put what was left in a savings account that I called 911. For emergency use only. The law firm paid my expenses to move to Texas. They also paid half of my lease. This permitted me to afford to live in a luxury apartment with security. Something I felt I needed living alone in a new city with no friends.

My son had studied agriculture in college and was raising cattle and horses. He loved knowing that he grew all his own feed and was well supplemented in his income.

I came back to the moment, and I realized I was pulling into my apartment complex. I had my own reserved parking spot. As I parked, I looked around me. The area was empty, but I spotted Gary the security guard walking down the sidewalk. He walked up as I was getting my groceries out.

"Well looks like you could use some help. Can I give you a hand?" Gary politely asks.

"Thank you, Gary. How is your day going?" I asked as I handed him two bags of groceries.

"So so. Are you coming to the Thanksgiving dinner tomorrow? The common room will be filled with lots of good food."

"I hadn't planned on it. It sounds like it might be fun though." We walked up the sidewalk to the doors of the apartment building.

I did not know anyone in the apartment. I liked keeping to myself. I loved living alone, and I was always weary of who I let know this information.

Gary continued talking about the dinner the next day. "You should try and stop by. My wife has made several pumpkin pies. You ought to at least come by for pie and coffee."

A teenage boy with a basketball opened the door for us and held it opened. I thanked him and walked over to the elevator and pushed the *up* button.

As I got on the elevator, I held the door with my foot to keep it from closing. I smiled at Gary reached for the bags he was holding and said,

"Thanks for your help Gary. You know pie is good. That sounds like good plan."

Chapter Five

Colin

It was good to be home. One of the perks of being an assistant to the Colonel was getting to take trips to other military bases. This trip had lasted fourteen days.

I arrived home around midnight last night. Today I was taking my first day of Thanksgiving break. Five days to rest up.

It had been a quiet morning, but now I could hear my upstairs neighbor. She must have just come home. I could faintly hear her radio.

The weather was nice, and my patio doors were open. I walked out onto the deck, and I tried to look up at the deck above me. My reward for being nosey was getting splashed with water. She must be watering plants.

I could hear the music louder out here but what sounded better was her voice as she sang along. A song about alcohol being the only thing that gets her.

I sat down in a deck chair and listened to her. I was imagining her dancing around on her deck with her watering can. Could be why she splashed water all over the side.

She was not a great singer, but that twang in her voice made the words cute and it was all I could do not to go up and knock on her door. I did owe her coffee or dinner.

I sat there long enough to talk myself out of it. I needed to get ready for poker night. It was my night to host. The guys would be dropping by in a few hours. I had a few questions for Gary.

Around 6:30 my doorbell buzzes letting me know some of the guys had arrived. I opened the door to Captain Robert Macleod. He was from Illinois but had made his home in a quaint suburban area outside San Antonio.

With him was Major Stephen Sommers. He was a San Antonio native. Both were pilots in the Air Force. We had been friends for years. Both men were happily married with several children between them. All their kids were in college now.

Robert had two sixers in his hands and Steve had bags of chips and pretzels. I shook hands with both, and they made themselves at home.

I was about to shut the door when Todd and Gary came in. Todd was a deputy Sheriff, and a brother-in-law to Gary. I met him through Gary and as the saying goes it never hurts to know a cop.

Gary came in carrying a pumpkin pie courtesy of his wife, Maria and Todd had a bag of tamales. Todd's wife Marla made the best tamales around. They always made sure I had plenty during the Holidays.

We were sitting around my poker table when my cell phone went off. It was Wyatt Dalton calling to say he was not going to make it tonight. Just as he was getting ready to leave his foreman had informed him his prize Appaloosa had started to foul. He had to hang around for the birth.

Wyatt was a retired Air Force Master Chief. He was also a native of Texas and lived in the Medina area. He owned a large ranch that stabled horses. He kept his horses as well as stabled horses for people who could not keep horses at their home.

Wyatt also hosted trail rides. One of my favorite pastimes was going out to his ranch for the trail rides. Sometimes they were day trips and sometimes several days of camping out.

I let the guys know it would just be the five of us. Todd shuffled the cards.

We had been playing a couple hours when we decided to take a break. I took this moment to ask Gary the questions I had been waiting to ask. We popped the tops on a couple beers, and I ask Gary,

"What's the scoop on my upstairs neighbor?"

Gary took a swig and said, "what scoop are we talking about?"

"Is she married, separated, divorced what?"

" None of the above. She is a widow. I think she said about three years when she moved in, so I would have to say about three and a half years now. She does not know anybody around here mostly keeps to herself. She is from Alabama and has a couple grown kids back there. I do not really know much just the basic info we need for emergency reason. She is a nice lady. She was sad a lot when she first moved in, but I notice in the last month or so she seems to smile more. So, is that the scoop we are talking about?"

Todd yelled break time was over and for us to come back to the table so he could lose the rest of his money. Yes, it was indeed turning out to be a good night for me. So far, I had won most every pot and my upstairs neighbor will single.

Two hours later as the guys were filing out the door Gary stopped and said, "see you in the common area for Thanksgiving dinner tomorrow?"

"Yes, I will be there".

"Be sure to hang around for dessert."

He winked and walked down the stairs. I shut the door and thought I cannot wait for dessert tomorrow. I will definitely reiterate my invite to dinner. Yes, indeed tomorrow will most definitely be sometime.

Chapter Six

Thanksgiving Day

Maggie

Thanksgiving Day. I had to drag myself out of bed. Sadness and depression trying to take over. I stumbled into my beautiful state of the art kitchen. Looking around I told myself my life was better. I need to shake off this melancholy that was consuming me.

I started the coffee machine then walked into my cozy living room. I turned on the television and scrolled through the channels until I found the Macy's Thanksgiving Day parade.

Back home we would be watching this as a family while waiting for dinner. Then we would watch the Alabama football game. We always rooted for Alabama Crimson Tide. As a matter of fact, they were playing later today.

I walked back into the kitchen and fixed myself a cup of coffee. Grabbing my tablet and my coffee I walked out onto my patio. It was going to be another beautiful day. The sun had already started to warm up the air.

I placed my coffee and tablet on the table and pulled up a chair nicely warmed from the sun. After a few sips of coffee, I clicked on my tablet and started a FaceTime with Allison. She answered after two rings as if she were just waiting for me to call.

"Good morning mama, are you outside?"

"Good morning baby girl, and yes I am. Look how beautiful the sun is shining."

I flipped my tablet around so the camera would show all around me.

"It is beautiful Mama; it is hard for me to wish you were here in the snow and cold when it is so nice there. I know you must enjoy it immensely."

"I do love the weather here in Texas. I am told it will get cold around February. I do miss the snow however, but not the cold."

We continued chatting and laughing about the weather and other tidbits. I could hear the baby crying in the background.

" Do you need to go so you can get Olivia?"

" No Mama, Joshua is getting her. You and I need to talk."

I took a deep breath and a sip of my coffee. Here it comes. She is going to berate me again for moving so far away. I mentally prepared myself for what was about to come.

" Mama, I want to tell you, well Joshua, Ben, Brittany and I were talking and well we want you to know we understand your need for a change. Fact is, it was moving so far away that bothered us the most. We worried about you. We were concerned about you all alone in a large city. If anything were to happen to you, we could not get to you quickly. But then Brittany reminded us that we could always fly out there in under two hours. Her dad owns a private plane. He could always get us out there if we needed to. We just miss you Mama so much. And well we have a surprise for you. We weren't going to tell you, but Brittney being the sensible one as usual said we need to let you know so you can be prepared."

I gulped down the rest of my coffee wondering what kind of surprise they had in store for me.

" Allison honey just tell me. Are you girls pregnant again?"

" Oh, hell no! We are done with baby making. The surprise is we are all going to fly out for a week during Christmas. Do you have room, or do we need to book a hotel?"

Wiping the tears off my face I said, " Oh wow, this is great news. I love this surprise. As for accommodations, I have a three-bedroom apartment. I did turn one of those rooms into a sewing room, but I can put a blow-up mattress in there for the boys. My sofa is also a Queen size bed. And I have Queen beds in both of my bedrooms. If y'all can decide who gets the bed and who gets the couch, we can make it work. I would rather have y'all here as much as possible so please decide to stay with me."

" I'll talk to everyone Mama, and let you know what we decide. We are thinking of coming on the twentieth and staying until the day after New Year's. Is that doable for you?"

" Yes, baby girl I'll make it doable. You have made me so happy. I was dreading today, but now I have something to look forward to. I will talk to you later this evening. Y'all have a great day I love you so much."

" I love you too Mama talk later."

I turned my tablet off set back in my chair. The smile on my face felt so foreign. For the first time in an exceedingly long time, I felt a semblance of happiness'. My children had finally forgiven me for leaving. And they were coming to Texas.! I had so much to do and only three weeks to do it in.

I picked up my coffee cup and went inside for a refill. While the coffee was brewing, I popped two slices of bread in the toaster. Standing in my kitchen waiting for the toaster to pop my mind was already tabulating what I needed to do.

I wanted to drive up to San Marcus tomorrow. Would that be advisable? Black Friday was both a great and bad day to shop. I could order online, but I like shopping around looking for the perfect gifts. I had already picked up a few items here and there. They were wrapped and ready to be shipped. Now they would go under my tree. My tree! I do not have a tree or decorations. I had left all that behind in Alabama.

I needed to make a list of items I needed to buy. I buttered my toast and took both toast and coffee back out on the patio.

I opened notes on my cell phone and started making my list. I did not realize how long I had sat outside until I heard faint music nearby. It was coming from the common area. The management folks were getting Thanksgiving dinner ready.

I had not planned on attending, but today I was so happy. I needed to go and speak to people. I wanted to get an idea where the best places to shop were. I would need to find a tree lot. Surely someone at the dinner would have answers for me. Of course, I could always just ask Gary, but I wanted no needed to try to be sociable. Maybe even make a friend or two.

I took my dishes back inside and rinsed them out in the sink and placed them in the dishwasher. I took a shower, fixed my hair, and dressed in a festive outfit. Well, festive for me meant blue jeans with boots and a Alabama, Crimson Tide jersey.

I loved this jersey; it was so soft and hugged my curves perfectly. I always tried to pull for the home team especially on days they were playing. So, wearing one of my Alabama shirts was the usual norm.

I looked at the clock and saw it was a quarter after noon. Tucking my cell phone in my back pocket I started my walk out to the common area. I was secretly hoping Brown eyes would be there.

Chapter Seven

Thanksgiving Day

Colin

Sleeping in was a rare treat. I was not normally a late riser. Even on my off days, I usually always got up early and took a run while it was still cool outside. But today was Thanksgiving and the guys stayed late last night.

As my coffee was brewing, I went out for my paper. I wondered what Miss beautiful was doing this morning. I wanted to go up and find out, but I did not want to appear overly ambitious.

I took my coffee and paper out on the patio. The sun was already beaming bright. Sipping my coffee, I concentrated on the headlines. I could hear voices above but could not really hear the conversation.

So, she had company today. Was it two female voices I heard? Why did it suddenly bother me to think she might be entertaining a man. Her life was her business not mine. But it did bother me. She was someone I really wanted to get to know better.

She did not appear the type to sleep around. She was more refined. Damn she was beautiful. It was hard to stop thinking about her. As I sat there half listening half daydreaming, I heard her patio door shut. At that moment, my cell phone beeped. I saw it was with Wyatt, so I answered.

" What's up bud? Happy Thanksgiving Day."

" Same to you LC."

Most all my close buddies referred to me as LC, short for Lieutenant Colonel.

" Hey, the wife wanted to know if you had somewhere to go today you know for the bird and all. She said to invite you out and bring a date if you want."

" That is exceedingly kind of Betty, but I already made plans. How is your horse doing? What did you get a colt or filly?"

"Aw man, we got the most beautiful little Filly you ever seen. Spitting image of her mama. Betty says she's not for sale we're keeping her."

"Congratulations can't wait to come out and meet her."

" Well come on out on Sunday. We can take a couple of old nags out for some exercise. It has been a few months since you were here. We can throw some steaks on the grill."

" Already scheduling it in my calendar. I'll be out early, around Ten."

"Great we will see you then talk later man."

"Yeah, later man."

As I ended my call, I heard my upstairs neighbor open her patio door. I could feel her presence up there. She was quiet. I could faintly hear her TV on. Sounded like the Macy's Thanksgiving Day Parade. Humm more info. She likes parades.

Maybe I would ask her to the Holiday River Parade on the Riverwalk. It was scheduled for late tomorrow afternoon and then the Lighting of the Lights on the River Walk.

I had a buddy who owned a bar on the Riverwalk. Several times in past years I had gone down and sat in his bar and watched the parade. I would have to call him and see if he could squeeze in a couple more seats. Yes, that is what I would do. Drinks, dinner, and a parade. Now to ask her.

Gary hinted around last night she might be coming out to the common area for dessert. I would strike up a conversation with her and see if she were interested in the downtown parade. If she appeared to be, I would ask her out.

I looked at the time. I should go in and take a shower. I had about an hour until I had to be in the common area for Thanksgiving dinner.

An hour later I walked into the common area. I had to give props to the management, the place was decorated very festively. Holiday music was blaring out of the overhead speakers. The pungent smells of turkey and dressings had my mouth watering. The aromatic smells of spices were intoxicating.

I spotted Gary and his wife Maria at a table set for eight. I grabbed a glass of tea and sauntered over to where the tables were laden down with platters of food. The dinner was catered but some of the tenants had brought out extra platters of food.

Gary spotted me and yelled for me to join him and Maria at their table. I walked over and shook his hand and hugged Maria. I thanked her for the pie from last night and told her it was extra delicious. She laughed and said she brought plenty more for dessert today.

I sat down and we discussed the food and the weather. I sipped my tea as more people walked in claiming seats and chatting with each other. Soon the room was full of people. Adults and children alike.

The chatter grew louder as folks walked around mingling and visiting with each other. Four more people sat down at our table.

I knew a lot of the tenants from previous get togethers that the apartment complex hosted. I saw a lot of new faces. All in all, it looked like it was going to be a great day to be thankful for.

As I chatted with the folks at my table I occasionally looked around. It was already noon and families with children had already lined up to fill plates for themselves and their children. As usual I had hung back and waited for the line to ease up. There was plenty of food, so I was not worried about not getting a good plateful. At that moment I overheard Gary's wife say.

" Gary, isn't that Maggie? The lady you told me about."

Gary stood up and said, " by golly it is, I'll have to go over an invite her to sit at our table".
As Gary sauntered off, Maria said. "Come on Colin lets go and get in line for some food."

I could not take my eyes off Maggie. Man, she was a looker. She appeared to be slightly nervous. I saw Gary walk up to her and she hugged him. She was smiling and shaking her head yes.

As Maria and I got closer to them Maggie looked at me and smiled. Was this what they called love at first sight? Because if I ever fell in love this moment would be how I hoped it would feel. Yes, I wanted more than anything to get to know her better. I could not take my eyes off her.

We both reached for plates at the same time. Her hand touched my hand. I felt the electricity run through my hand up my arm and down to my gut. I pulled my hand back and said,

    " Ladies first".

Chapter Eight

Thanksgiving Day

Maggie

As I stepped inside the common room I was filled with an overwhelming case of the jitters. I was so out of my comfort zone, and I was letting fear take over. Was I doing the right thing? Is making friends a good idea? As it is not many people know I lived alone. I always thought I was safer by not making my living conditions known. Was I allowing paranoia to consume me again. But what kind of life was that? People need people. Right? No one should live their lives in fear.

That had been my life for so many years. Gregory had brainwashed me all those years ago, berating and accusing me. I lived in constant fear of what he might do or say. Always I would have to pretend in front of the children and family. I never had any friends except for Missy. I could just hear her now.

" *Girl march in there with your sexy ass smile and make some friends.*"

So, I did.

I walked more inside and looked around. So many people. All laughing and having a great time. I saw the line at the food table. As I walked in that direction, I suddenly heard my name.

"Maggie, you decided to come. It's so good to see you."

Gary pulled me into a hug. I smiled at him. Shaking my head, I said

"Yes, I just couldn't bring myself to eat a frozen Turkey dinner with all this delicious food just a few steps away."

He laughed and said, "you must sit at our table. Oh, here comes my wife Maria and Colin. Have you met Colin? He is a Lieutenant Colonel in the Air Force. A great guy."

Gary left to join his wife in line. I followed him and when I reached for a plate a hand touched mine. It was Colin's hand. He quickly removed his hand and said,

"Ladies first."

I smiled at him and said,

"Why thank you Sir."

I grabbed a plate and some silverware and joined Gary and Maria in line. There was so much food. The tables were loaded down with platters of Turkey and Ham. Bowls full of dressing and stuffing. Cranberry sauce of every variety. There was a huge pot of Tamales. Large bowls of salad and every dressing you could think of. Three different types of gravy were in cute gravy bowls. Rolls, cornbread, and biscuits lay beneath warmers. I saw several dishes I was not sure of, but they did look delicious.

As I loaded my plate with Turkey dressing and yams, I looked behind me. I noticed Colin had two plates. When he saw me looking at his plates, he said.

"Not enough room for a little of everything on one plate."

I laughed and said, "you're so right but I'll stick with the Thanksgiving dinner originals."

I added a few of two different kinds of green beans to my plate. I skipped over the four types of potato salad and settled for the mashed potatoes instead. I poured giblet gravy over my food and placed several spoonsful or cranberry sauce on top of the dressing. Skipping the salad and the bread, I followed Gary and Maria to the table. I took the chair on Marias left. She took my hand and said,

"Hello Maggie dear, my name is Maria. This lug is my wonderful husband. He speaks very highly of you. We're just so glad you joined us today."

I squeeze her hand. "I thought it was time I started attending the festive celebrations you have here. This food looks so delicious. Is it ok if I bless my food first."

"Of course, dear. Do you mind waiting until the others Join us?"

I smiled and shook my head yes. Four more people sat down at our table leaving one chair open beside me. I looked around the room wondering who would be sitting next to me when Gary laughed and said,

"Hey Colin, you need some help there?"

Colin let Gary take the two glasses of Tea from his hands and set his two plates down next to mine.

"I hope you don't mind I grabbed you a drink when I got mine. I notice you didn't get any before you sat down."

I accepted a glass of tea from Gary and said, "thank you, Colin, how thoughtful."

Colin pulled out the chair next to me and sat down. Maria lightly tapped her tea glass, "now everyone is seated let us join hands and give thanks for this bounty. Maggie, would you mind saying grace."

I took Colin's and Marie's hands bowed my head and closed my eyes.

"Heavenly father we have gathered here today to share a meal of Thanksgiving. Thank you for bringing us together and thank you for the delicious food. Heavenly Father bless those around us and those who prepared the food. Guide our mealtime conversations and steer our hearts to your purpose for our lives. To you I give all the glory in Jesus' name Amen.

Maria squeezed my hand and said, "that was just beautiful Maggie. Amen and Amen and let's eat."

As Colin released my hand, I looked over at him. He smiled at me and said, "nice prayer thank- you."

The conversation around the table was light and witty as everyone ate and discussed the different foods. A server was walking around refilling tea and water glasses. I was enjoying myself immensely. One of the ladies at the table ask where I was originally from .I told her Alabama. One of the guys said it was obvious as I was wearing a Roll Tide Jersey. I glanced down at my shirt and said,

   "Yep, Roll Tide."

Clearing his throat Gary asked. "Do you enjoy watching football."

   "Yes, I enjoy College and high school football. I don't much care for pro ball of any kind."

Wiping her mouth Maria said, "you're not a Spurs Fan?"

I rolled my eyes and said, "Oh no."

This got a laugh around the table with someone saying I should keep that information on the down low around San Antonio.

Gary asked, "Which teams do root for."

" Alabama Crimson Tide and whoever is playing against the Vols."

That got a huge laugh out of Colin. "I take it you're not a Tennessee Vols fan?"

I laughed and said, "I don't really care, but that is a joke around Alabama. Alabama and Tennessee have been archrivals for such a long time."

"They are paying later today are you watching?"

"That is my plan."

One of the other women at the table asked,

"Have you been down to the river walk."

"No, but a few coworkers invited me to go watch the parade tomorrow."

Colin said, "so, you have plans to go tomorrow?"

"No, I turned them down but wished I hadn't . I really love parades."

Colin reached over and picked up my plate along with his and said, " I'm going after pie and coffee. May I bring you some?"

"Please, that would be great. Thank you."

Colin returned with two slices of pumpkin pie and two cups of coffee. I smiled and said thank you. Taking a bite of pie, I moaned with pleasure.

"Oh, my but this pie is divine."

Maria laughed, "thank you."

I quickly swallowed my big bite and said, "you made this."

She nodded her head, "yes."

"I must have the recipe."

"I'll send to you by Gary next week."

I thanked her.

Everyone but Colin got up and left the table to get dessert leaving us alone. Colin cleared his throat and said, "do you remember I asked you to go for a drink or coffee or maybe grab some dinner sometime?"

"Yes, I do remember".

"If you aren't busy maybe we could go tomorrow evening downtown to watch the parade and the lighting of the lights. We could grab some dinner too."

"I appreciated your offer, but I have plans to do some Black Friday Christmas shopping."

Maria arrived back at our table and as she sat back down, she said,

"Oh, but dear you really must go to the parade."

"Well, I had planned to drive up to San Marcus to shop."

Maria said, "really. my sister and I are going up early. We plan to leave around 5:00 AM. Would you like to join us? We will be back by one or two then you can go with Colin to the parade."

I looked at Colin said, "well OK then I accept your offer. I would be pleased to join you."

I Turned to Maria and said, "and "I will be glad to go with you too. Where should I meet you?"

"We will pick you around 5:00 AM."

I exchanged cell numbers with both Maria and Colin. She said she would call in the morning when she was outside.

Colin said. "I'll be up around three to get you. Parking is difficult downtown, so I'll have a rideshare ready to pick us up."

I finished my coffee wiped my mouth and said, "I really enjoyed myself today, but I do need to run. My grandkids will be waiting for me to FaceTime with them."

Colin stood and said, "may I walk you home."

I gladly accepted. I hugged Maria and Gary and told Maria I could not wait until our shopping adventure tomorrow.

Chapter Nine

Maggie

So far today had been one of the best days I had had since moving to Texas. The trip to the outlet mall in San Marcus with Maria and her sister Marla had been very productive. We arrived at our first store thirty minutes before it opened and was incredibly lucky the line was short. I found matching PJ'S for everyone. The boys may try to get out of wearing them, but the girls were going to love them. I got all nine of us a pair and I booked a photographer to come by my apartment on Christmas Eve for a family portrait.

At the baby store I found several cute outfits for the children. At the cowboy store I got cowboy hats and boots for all of Benjamin's family. For Allison's family I found the newest gaming system with all the perks. I bought different Texas T-shirts for all of them also. I picked up a lot of decorations for my apartment. Tomorrow I planned to go shopping for lights and a tree and more decorations.

The volunteers from the Children's Hospital had set up a gift-wrapping kiosk near the entrance to the mall. I love wrapping gifts, but it felt right getting all my gifts wrapped. It was a little pricey but well worth it. The proceeds were for a children's Christmas charity. The ladies and I had drove up to San Marcus in Marla's van. That was lucky for us because we had it loaded down before coming back to San Antonio.

I had just over an hour to be ready for my date with Colin. I showered and did my makeup. I struggled with what kind of outfit I should wear. After going through almost all my clothes I decided on black jeans and boots and a Christmas sweater. Satisfied with my choice I was just adding a splash of my favorite Cologne when my doorbell alerted me to the door. I opened the door to find Colin dressed in jeans and a red sweater. He smiled his sexy smile and said,

"Well OK beautiful, you ready".

I grabbed my over the shoulder bag and said, "why yes I am."

On the elevator ride down to the main lobby we chatted about how our day had been. He laughed as I told him about the matching PJS I had purchased. On our ride downtown we kept up the small talk I asked questions about the river walk.

Colin answered every question like a tour guide. He was so comfortable to be around. Traffic was moving slow, and Colin said it would be worse the closer we got downtown. I told him it was smart to get a ride share . He said yes because parking will be nearly impossible.

The ride share dropped us off in front of the entrance to the river walk. It was so crowded already. Colin said we were expected at his friend's bar, so we walked down the sidewalk until we arrived at the bar.

Colin introduced me to his friend Dominic Gaffney, owner operator of Gaffney Bar and Grill. Dominic guided us upstairs to a table outside on the portico. We had perfect seats for the parade. Dominic informed Collin that the drinks and food were on him tonight. Colin tried to argue but Dominic would not have it. He motioned for a waiter to our table and said he would see us in a few.

Colin asked what I wanted to drink. I ordered a frozen Margarita, and he ordered a Scotch on the rocks for himself. When the waiter returned with our drinks, he brought a huge tray loaded down with appetizer samplers .

As we ate, we heard the beginning of the parade starting. I pulled my phone out so I could video parts of the parade to show the grandkids.

Colin was very attentive. I told him where I was from, my family and my job. He in turn told me about his family and his job. Before we knew it three hours had passed.

He asked if I would like to walk the Riverwalk. It would soon be time for the Christmas lights to come on . I eagerly said yes.

As we walked out Colin and I said goodbye to Dominic. Colin thanked him for his gracious hospitality and shook his hand. Dominic slapped Colin on the back and winked at me and told us not to be strangers.

We walked down the sidewalk. I found myself enjoying being with Colin. He was extremely smart and well informed. He made me feel amazingly comfortable. He was the perfect gentleman.

Occasionally I felt his hand on my the small of my back as he guided me a certain way down the walk. When the lights came on and you could barely hear yourself .

Everyone was yelling and clapping. It was so beautiful it brought tears to my eyes. I looked at Colin and he wiped a tear from my cheek and said,

"Are you ok ?"

"Yes, Colin I am, it's just so beautiful and I guess I'm just a little melancholy."

I retrieved a tissue from my purse, and we continued our walk.

We found ourselves back out on the street and I noticed our rideshare. Colin must have text him as we walked. It was such a wonderful afternoon and evening and I hated to see it come to an end.

Colin asked if I was hungry. I told him I was famished. He instructed the rideshare to a famous steakhouse.

So far, the evening was going great.

We arrived at the steakhouse and Collin, and I got out. When we walked in, we were immediately seated. We ordered our drinks and Colin asked if I needed a minute to look over the menu. I shook my head no. I smiled up at the waitress and ordered,

" I would like a half rack of ribs, sauce on the side. A fully loaded baked potato and a house salad with ranch dressing, also on the side."

Colin smiled at me and spoke to the waitress,

" I'll have the same thing but with a full rack of ribs and with nothing on the side. Load it all on top."

The waitress smiled at Colin and said,
"You got it sir."

I noticed a few women checked out Colin as we were being seated. The waitress I am sure was just as impressed with his looks.

The juke box was playing a country song and I found myself humming along. Colin asked about the song, and I told him it was one of my favorites.

The waitress brought our drinks and salads and we chatted about music and TV shows while we enjoyed our food.

The next two hours flew by. By the time Colin walked me to the door of my apartment I felt I knew all I needed to know about Colin. I unlocked my door and turned to Colin,

"Thank you for a wonderful afternoon and dinner."

He reached for my hand and said,

"It was the most fun I have had in years."

He kissed my hand and his breath on my fingers sent shivers through my body. He winked at me said,

" Goodnight, can I call you sometime?"

"Yes, please do."

I shut the door and grabbed my cell phone out of my bag. As I shook off my boots, I was already dialing Missy's number. I had so much to say.

Chapter Ten

Maggie

I turned off my computer and checked to see if I had finished all I needed to do. My Monday morning To Do List was taped to my keyboard. I reached for my purse and my cell phone.

I had a text from Colin. I quickly texted back that I was just leaving work and yes, I would love to go to dinner with him.

As I rode the elevator to the garage, I could not help but smile. It had been a week since our first date. Colin had called almost every evening and texted several times a day. I was looking forward to seeing him again.

On my ride home I thought about what I would wear. By the time I had pulled into the parking lot of the apartment complex I had decided on a dress with heels.

After all those years of wearing homemade house dresses with my hair in a ponytail I loved getting dressed up.

I always wore my hair up in a nice style for work, but otherwise I wore it down. Once a month I treated myself to a spa day. I would get a Mani/Pedi along with hair and facial treatments. My girl at the spa always complemented me on my complexion. I told her I had always used a face cream. It was something I started in my late teens. Because of that I did have great skin and no wrinkles. I never smoked and it was only after Gregory died that I had become a social drinker.

In the process of trying to find me, I had found I still had plenty of life left in me. I was not ever going to go back to that person Gregory had made.

I showered and dressed for my date with Colin. My dress was made from green chiffon. It had a scoop neckline with an A- line skirt that just hit my knees. The short sleeves were tailored with small Pearl buttons on the side. The waist fit snug. The dress fit me perfectly. Looking at myself in the full-length mirror I smiled. Was that really me? Missy was right I did not look like an old grandma. I looked like a sexy Nana.

I added Pearl stud earrings and a small Pearl covered cross on a gold chain.

The days were warm enough for short sleeves, but the nights tended to be a bit cooler, so I added a beautiful white shawl to my outfit. My two-inch Mary Jane Heels completed my outfit. I touched up my lipstick and grabbed a small purse just big enough to carry my wallet and cellphone.

Colin texted to say he was on his way up. I waited just inside my door. I was a nervous wreck and was beginning to second guess my choice of outfits, when my buzzer alerted me that Colin had arrived. Taking a deep breath of air, I opened my door.

Colin was dressed in black dress slacks with a Gray button-down collared shirt and a pullover sweater that was Gray with black pinstripes. He was so handsome. As we stood there staring at each other, Colin suddenly took my hand and said,

"Wow, just wow."

"Am I overdressed Colin, should I change?"

"Maggie you are a vision and no you look just perfect." .

I smiled and slowly let my breath out .

"You look nice too Colin. Thank you for inviting me to dinner."

Colin wrapped my hand around his arm and lead me to the elevator.

When we arrived at the parking lot Colin opened the door to his truck and helped me inside. He got in on the driver side and said to me,

"Do you like Thai food ?"

Smiling over at him I said, "I have never had it before, but I am always up to trying something new."

Looking me over he I saw a twinkle in his eyes as he said, "I was thinking we could get Thai, but now I'm thinking different, I know of a great place over in La Cantera."

"Colin," anywhere will be simply fine ".

On the drive to the restaurant, we talked about our week. He apologized for not asking me out sooner, but he had already made plans for the past weekend and his job had him working late most days. I told him no worries my week had been full also.

At the restaurant there was a ten-minute wait for the table Colin wanted, so we sat at the bar and sipped on glasses of wine. I had never had the Cabernet Sauvignon before and found the taste delightful.

It was not long before a waitress informed Colin his table was ready. I loved the atmosphere of the restaurant . It was quite fancy and not in the least noisy. Our table was located in a quiet secluded corner. The overhead music was soft and lovely.

The waitress handed us menus and said she would be right back for our orders. Colin told the waitress to bring a fresh bottle of the wine we were drinking.

She returned shortly and we placed our order. I ordered a salad and a shrimp scampi entree with assorted veggies. Colin ordered a salad and a T-bone steak with French fries. As we sat waiting on our food Colin reached for my hand and played with my fingers. It had a calming effect on me. We talked and talked about everything and nothing.

When our food arrived, we talked mostly about the food. Colin kept filling our glasses with the wine. I loved talking to Colin and was quickly falling for him. I loved that we agreed on so many topics. After dinner Colin ordered us both coffee and a creme' Brule for dessert. We sat for hours and had several more cups of coffee.

I excused myself to the powder room and Colin got the check. When I returned, he took my hand and led me out to his truck. Once again, he opened my door but before he helped me into the truck he leaned in and said,

"Please don't get mad but I'm going to kiss you."

He took my face in both of his hands and his lips just grazed mine. It was the sweetest kiss I had ever had. When Colin stepped back, he took my hand and helped me into the truck. I turned to him and touched his face with my hand and smiled.

"Colin that was so sweet "

He kissed the palm of my hand then closed the door.

On the drive back to our apartment complex he held my hand and we talked about what our weekend plans were.

I told him I wanted to find a Christmas tree farm. He said he knew one of the best places around to get a fresh tree.

"If you would like I can take you on Saturday afternoon,"

"I would love that. I wasn't sure how I was going to fit a tree in my car."

We arrived back at our apartments. I felt a sadness that our perfect evening would soon be over. Colin opened my door and helped me out of his truck. I was always amazed of his gentlemanly actions. He took my hand and we walked slowly from the parking lot to the lobby I felt as if I was walking on air.

On the elevator ride to my apartment, he continued to hold my hand. At my door I was just about to invite him in for coffee, but before I could speak, he pulled me up close, his hot breath burning my lips as he slowly lowered his lips to mine. When our lips touched, the electricity that shot through me ignited a fire deep inside my soul. The kiss only lasted a short minute but left me wondering what more there was. Colin took a step back and said,

"goodnight sweet Maggie, see you tomorrow "

Then he took the steps down to his apartment.

I just stood there mesmerized, my fingers lightly touching my lips.

Coming back to my senses I walked into my apartment and took off my shoes. I removed my dress and hung it in the closet. I put on my night gown and went into the bathroom to wash my face and brush my teeth. I felt like I was moving in slow motion. I crawled into bed and reach for my cell phone.

Missy answered on the first ring.

"Tell me everything" she blurted out quickly.

I scooted down in bed and told Missy everything from the moment he picked me up until he brought me home .

Chapter Eleven
Colin

The alarm ringing woke me from a dream. In the dream I had met the most charming, beautiful woman ever. But it wasn't a dream. She was real. I could still taste her kiss. I could still feel her body tremble as I held her in my arms. I climbed out of bed and headed to the shower. Thinking about her smile, I turned the water to cold.

I was just finishing my third Cup of coffee when my cell went off. It was Wyatt.

"Hey bud, what's going on?"

"Not much LC, just thought I'd call and see how your date went."

"What, are we in high school? What do you mean how it went?"

Wyatt was laughing, and I could hear Betty in the background saying,

"Ask him."

"Well LC, Betty wants to meet the lady who got you back in the dating world."

"Put Betty on."

"Hello Colin, really how was your second date?"

"Hello Betty, the date was great. I am taking her to find a Christmas tree today. And before you ask yes, I will bring her out soon. How's that filly doing?"

"Oh Colin, she is beautiful and doing very well. You promise to bring her, soon, right?"

"Yes Betty, I will. Bye Betty."

"Bye Colin"

I texted Maggie to see if she was ready to go. She texted back she would be ready in five minutes. I looked at my watch and walked out my door. Taking the stairs two at a time I stood outside her door.

When five minutes had passed, I rang the bell. Maggie opened her door and my stomach knotted. How beautiful she was. I reached for her, and she naturally slipped into my arms. I kissed her soft and slow. Her hands on my chest . This just felt so natural. She was meant for my arms. We fit together perfectly. Reluctantly I pulled back.

"You ready to go get a tree?"

She smiled and said, "yes."

We drove up to Fredericksburg. I had heard they had the best Christmas tree lot. The trip took a couple hours and I held her hand all the way. My thumb constantly caressing hers. She talked about her children coming in a few weeks.

"I need to get a couple small cots and a couple pack and plays for the grand babies to sleep in."

"I can help you with that. We could get them today if you want to."

She smiled and squeezed my hand.

We arrived in Fredericksburg "shall we grab some lunch first?"

"Yes, I'm famished.

We found a great little place on Main Street. We set side-by-side in the booth and every so often I would lean over and kiss her. She was very shy but seemed to enjoy the kissing. I loved holding her hand and her smell was intoxicating.

We talked more about her children. She told me about how her son had bought her farm and her daughter was a registered nurse. I could hear the proud mother in her as she spoke.

She talked about her two grandsons and how remarkably bright they were and how the two grand girls had just stared walking. She smiled a lot and every so often a soft laugh would escape. Every time she laughed, I felt something inside. I could honestly say I had never felt like that before.

After lunch we shopped around several different stores and finally the Christmas tree lot.

Three hours later we headed back to San Antonio. She had found a nice full tree and I had promised I would help set it up for her.

The back of my truck was loaded down with all her purchases.

She was a very independent woman. I offered to buy her the tree, but she said no. She appreciated the offer, but she could pay for it herself. She then kissed my cheek and said.

"Colin, you offered to drive me up here. Go to all the different stores with me and then offered to help me set the tree up that is really enough thank you."

I smiled at her, "just to spend the day with you was more than worth it."

When we arrived back at our apartments, I texted one of the teenage boys who I was mentoring to come out to the truck. He came out with a couple of his buddies and helped carry everything inside for her. When everything was carried in, they turned to leave. She tried to pay the boys, but they would not take her money. They were good kids, and I would make sure they were paid well later. She Invited me to stay, and I accepted.

Her apartment was very cozy. You could tell a female lived there.

While she slipped off to another room to get the tree stand, I walked around her living room. She had lots of pictures of her children and grandchildren. I noticed two large pictures of her two children with their families. The two families were so similar. Her son and daughter looked almost like Twins. You could tell the grandsons and granddaughters were remarkably close in age. I was sure there was a cute story behind that.

She came back into the room and handed the tree stand to me. She had already arranged a place to set her tree up. We went to work on the tree. Me on the floor, her holding the tree and giving advice. After several tries, we finally had the tree the way she wanted.

I asked to use her restroom to wash my hands. When I returned to her living room, she handed me a glass of wine and told me to have a seat. I sat on her sofa, and she chose the chair next to me. I told her she had a beautiful place. She smiled and said it was home.

Suddenly she stood up and said, "Oh, my goodness Colin, you must be starved."

I laughed and took her hand and pulled her down on the sofa beside me. "I'll order a pizza and maybe we can hang your lights on the tree." She agreed and I placed a pizza order.

She was sitting close to me, so I put my arm around her, and she leaned in for a kiss. I kept the kisses soft and sensual. I was not ready to rush her with passionate kisses yet. I wanted to take it slow and easy. We sat there kissing for a while. Reluctantly I pulled back and I asked her about the two pictures on the wall. As she sipped her wine and held my hand, she told me the story.

Her children were eleven months apart. They both started school at the same time. They shared the same friends all through school. Her son Benjamin was best friends with Joshua. Allison was best friends with Brittany. It was not until they graduated high school and had left for college that the four best friends fell in love. After two years in college, they had a double wedding. Brittany and Allison discovered they were both pregnant and they were due at the same time. The boys were born one week apart. She said she helped with the boys so both girls could finish college. A year after they all four graduated college both girls gave birth again. The baby girls were born hours apart . \

Maggie laughed and said,

"It was so uncanny. They are the talk of the town. But both families are well respected pillars of the community and members of the church."

We hung the lights, ate the pizza, and drank more wine. She had music playing on her Alexa. Romantic Christmas music from the fifties.

When a slow Christmas song came on, I took her hand and pulled her close and we slow danced in front of her tree. I buried my face in her hair and took a deep breath. She smelled so good, and her body felt so soft.

She was softly humming and when the song ended, she lifted her face to mine, and I kissed her again. I pulled her closer and she caressed my neck with her fingers. We stood there kissing lost in each other. I knew I had to stop so I pulled back took both of her hands in mine. I kissed both palms and whispered,

"it's late I should go."

She shook her head yes and walked me to the door. Her eyes were glazed over, and I could feel the passion flowing from her body. At the door I kissed her one last time and said,

"Talk to you soon."

She just nodded her head and watched as I walked down the stairs.

Chapter Twelve

Maggie

I wrapped a light blanket around me grabbed my cell phone and my coffee and went out to the patio. I was fast learning the Texas weather.

The days were usually warm, but morning almost always was cooler. I enjoyed the fresh air in the mornings.

As I sat and sipped my coffee my mind wandered back over the last three weeks.

I had a great time with Colin in Fredericksburg. He was so helpful getting my tree and the beds for the kids. At the tree lot we walked forever until I found the perfect tree. It was nice being with someone who was patient with me.

At the big box store we found sturdy cots that would accommodate two rowdy boys. The pack and plays were on sale, and I knew they would only be used this one time, so I planned to donate them later.

I fell in love with the area around Fredericksburg. Colin and I discussed going back someday. I told him I would love to visit the Natural Museum of the Pacific war and the Pioneer Museum. He promised to take me back again soon as the weather was warmer.

I missed Colin.

He had been gone for almost three weeks. He was in Nevada at Nelis Air Force Base. He told me he took trips often for his job, but he called me every night. When he could he texted me during the day.

The week after our trip to Fredericksburg and before he left, we spent as much time as possible together. Of course, we both worked so lunches and dinners were all we could manage.

He was like no one I had ever met before. Gregory was the only man I had ever been with but, he had never made me feel the way Colin did.

All we had done so far was kiss and hold hands, but we talked a lot. He was genuinely interested in what I had to say. I knew I was falling for him. Falling like I never believed I ever would. Thinking about Colin made me burn with desire. A deep heated passion that reached my deepest core. Was it possible at my age to feel sensual desire again?

Lost in my thoughts of Colin I reluctantly came back to the present. The kids would be here tomorrow. I had everything ready for their arrival. I had moved everything in my sewing room out of the way and set both cots up for the boys. The two pack in plays were already set up and ready for the girls. I had gone through every inch of my apartment and baby proofed everything.

My plan was to go grocery shopping later today to stock the fridge and pantry. Colin would be back Monday. How was I going to explain him to Benjamin and Allison? This had me anxious.

Last night when Colin asked me on the phone about their arrival, I told him my concerns. He was so sweet and so understanding. He said maybe we should lay low while the kids were here. I told him I wanted him to meet the kids. But I was not sure if they would understand.

I still had to work three days after the kids arrived. Colin said he would meet me for lunch everyday as usual on those three days, but he would not intrude when my family was here.

My cell phone beeped, and I saw it was Colin. A huge smile lit of my face and a thrill went thru my body.

"Good morning Colin."

"Good morning beautiful are you busy?"

"No, just sitting here procrastinating going shopping."

" What time is the kids flight tomorrow."

"They arrive at 4:15 in the afternoon. I reserved two cars for them and gave them the address here. I Cannot go pick them up in my car it is too small. I arranged with management to give me two extra parking spots outside. I gave Allison the gate code and the parking numbers. They promised to call when they pulled in so I can walk out to meet them."

"You're excited to see them grandkids aren't you."

"Yes, Colin I am. It has been so long. What about you. What time do you get back?"

"Late tomorrow night. I miss you."

"Oh Colin, I miss you too."

We talked for a while then I went inside to get dressed to go shopping .

Sunday afternoon came and I was very excited . The kids would arrive any moment . I had dinner ready for them. All my gifts were wrapped and hidden in my closet. I would bring them out on Christmas Eve so the children would know Santa found them in Texas. Allison beeped my cell to let me know they were here. I hurried down the stairs to greet them. Allison was the first to see me. She ran up to me and pulled me into a tight hug.

"Oh, Mama it's so good to see you again."

She backed up and looked at me slyly.

"Mama you look different. What have you done?"

Before I could answer her Benjamin was hugging me. Joshua walked up carrying Olivia and holding Logans hand. I picked up Logan and hugged and kissed him. He hugged me back tightly and said,

"I missed you so so much, Nana."

"Oh baby, Nana has missed you too so much."

I reluctantly put him down and reached for Olivia. She was so sweet and let me kiss and hug her. I handed Olivia back to Joshua as Brittney came up and hugged me. She handed me Sophia. I kissed and hugged her chubby cheeks then handed her to Benjamin. Benji grabbed my leg and I bent down to hug him.

" Hi Nana, I miss you. We rode on a plane. It was cool."

I laughed and kissed his cheeks.

"I missed you too buddy and I bet it was cool."

Everyone was talking and making comments about the complex. Joshua and Benjamin left to go unload their luggage. I took both boys by the hand and started walking toward my apartment. They were both talking nonstop about the plane ride. They both wanted to know.

"Why don't Texas have snow. Will Santa come to Texas Nana."

It was going to be a fun ten days. As Happy as I was to have my family with me Colin was always right there in the front of my mind .

And I could not stop smiling when I thought of him. I noticed every so often Brittney would look at me and smile like she knew I had a secret, but she never said anything. I knew deep down she knew. I do not know how she knew, but one thing was for sure I was going to have to tell my secret soon.

\\

Chapter Thirteen

Maggie

Christmas was over and I had not seen Colin for a few days. He texted me often and I would call him late at night after everyone was in bed.

He texted me one day to ask if I was going to the New Year's Eve gala the apartment complex was having. I told him yes, that Gary and Maria's two twin granddaughters were going to babysit for us. We would all six be attending. He said for me to be prepared because he was going to dance with me. I told him I was looking forward to it. I had decided to tell my family about Colin. I just was not sure when. Allison, Brittany, and I were going today to buy dresses for the dance. Benjamin and Joshua were taking the children to the park next door to the complex.

The girls and I were walking to my car when I saw Colin getting out of his truck. He waved, and I smiled at him. I motioned him over. I took a deep breath and slowly let it out.

"Allison, Brittany, I would like you to meet Lieutenant Colonel Colin Douglas. Colin, my daughter Allison and my daughter-in-law Brittany."

He shook both girls' hands. I told him we were on our way dress shopping for the dance. He turned to the girls and said,

"Well, I'll let you get on your way. It was a pleasure to meet you ladies, Maggie save me a dance?"

"Of course, Colin, see you at the dance."

As I was driving to the mall, Allison asked me about Colin. I told her he lived in the same building one floor below me. She said he was hot for an old man. I laughed and said,

"Oh really".

Brittany inquired if I knew anything about him. I slowly inhaled and said that I met him at Thanksgiving dinner at the complex. I informed them he was a Lieutenant Colonel in the Air Force. That seemed to be enough info to satisfy them, and the conversation turned to dresses and shoes.

Hours later we had found our beautiful outfits. My dress was a black floor length with a round neckline. It had short sleeves with an illusion lace yoke embellished with sequins. The front side slit that reached to my thigh was a bit daring, but it looked amazing on me. It hugged all my curves in just the right places. I had purchased three-inch spike black heels with crisscross straps and a cute White faux fur Bolero jacket. Alison was in shock as she had never seen me dressed like this before. Brittany hid her smile, but I could tell by her look that she was getting very suspicious.

On the way home we stopped for some Texas barbecue for dinner. Colin and I had dined there once, and I had fallen in love with the cream corn.

Allison made remarks about how well I could drive in the busy city. I told her it was easy as long as I had GPS . They both laughed .

Brittany asked me when I had bought my car. I had driven out to Texas in a Chevy minivan. It was paid for so a month after I started my new job, I traded it in on a brand-new Black Lexus SUV . I loved my new car and I told Brittany when I had traded. She remarked I had good taste in cars. Allison said they had just purchased a new van themselves and said she would show me pics later. I asked Brittany was she still driving her Jeep. She said,

"Yes, ma'am always."

Back at the apartment the boys were watching a ball game. They were excited to see us return with food.

I carried my dress into my bedroom and hung it in my closet. Colin texted me and I texted back that I would slip out and meet him in the laundry room.

I gathered up a basket of laundry and told the kids I would be right back I was going to run down to the laundry room. Allison offered to go with me and help. I told her no need just feed the kids and that I would not be long.

I had just shut the lid on the washer when I felt Colin behind me. He put his arms around me and pulled me back against him.

I lean my head back against his shoulders and he kissed me on the side of my neck. He whispered in my ear how much he missed me. I whispered back that I missed him too.

We stood like that for a few minutes. I turned around and he pulled me into his arms and kissed me. I wanted to stay like that forever and told him so. He said it was just a few more days and that right now, my family was more important.

Once again, I was amazed at how selfless he was. I took his hand and said come to the apartment with me. He asked if I was sure, and I said yes just to meet my son. Maybe if they knew I had a good neighbor it might help them feel I was safer. It never hurt to know I had good friends to help me in time of need. I squeezed his hand and we walked to the elevator.

Inside the elevator he pulled me into his arms for one more kiss. Just as the doors opened, we stepped apart.

I opened the door to my apartment and found Olivia walking in the foyer. I picked her up and snuggled her to me. Allison walked in and was shocked to see Colin directly behind me.

"Honey, I ran into Colin in the laundry room. Remember I told you he lives directly below me, so I asked him to come up for some bar-b-que. With the nine of us stomping around up here the least we could do is offer him a glass of wine and some brisket."

By this time, we had walked into the living room. Joshua turned the television sound down and he and Benjamin stood up. I introduced them both to Colin. Benjamin asked how we knew each other, and I said,

"I met Colin at the Thanksgiving dinner the complex held. I occasionally run into him around the complex. Benjamin, we are neighbors and I thought you might sleep better knowing someone in the United States Air Force lived in my building if I ever needed help."

Joshua said. "Well, I know Allison will be. She worries constantly about you mom."

I told Colin to have a seat and I stepped out to the kitchen to fix us both plates. Brittany walked into the kitchen carrying Sofia. She smiled at me, and I winked at her. She turned and walked back out.

I took the plates of food and the glasses of wine
and walked back into the living room. Colin stood and
accepted a plate and a glass of wine. I sat down in my
chair, and we watched the game and enjoyed the food .

The boys seemed to be enjoying their conversation
with Colin. I still was not ready to tell them about us.
But I felt when the time came, they would accept Colin
in my life.

Chapter Fourteen

New Year's Eve

As my family and I entered the room the girls were immediately excited.

The common room was elegantly decorated in a formal atmosphere. There were hundreds of twinkling lights strung from floor to ceiling. The twinkling lights crisscrossing in every direction all along the ceiling. The black, gold, and silver-colored balloons covered the dance floor. The band was set up in a corner and was already blasting away. There were huge disco balloon balls hanging from the ceiling waiting for midnight to drop confetti to the floor. Three dozen tables set for six each were decorated with black tablecloths. Gold candles trimmed in silver and surrounded by flowers as centerpieces. Gold and silver glitter sprinkled everywhere.

A table was set up at the entrance for party guest to sign in and collect party favors. A bar was on one side of the room and a buffet table was set up on the other wall.

two sets of French doors were open at the back and tables and chairs were set up for those in need of fresh air throughout the night. The whole atmosphere of the room was exciting and at first glance one could tell a good time would be had by all.

Allison and Brittney both grab the hands of their husbands and hit the dance floor. I wandered around the room until I saw Gary and Maria talking to another couple. I walked up to them just as Maria spotted me.

"Oh, Maggie dear there you are. We are so pleased you were able to join us tonight. The Twins have talked nonstop all day about watching the children tonight."

Hugging Maria I said, "yes, they were right on time and as we were leaving both boys had them on the floor playing with trucks, cars and the train set."

The band switched to a slow song and Gary took Maria's hand and said,

"Excuse us, Maggie. Come along my dear they're playing our song."

Maria giggled like a schoolgirl and followed Gary out to the dance floor.

I stood there watching my adult children as they were slow dancing out on the floor. I had a huge smile on my face. I was so engrossed with watching the dancers I did not notice Collin had appeared at my side holding two glasses of champagne.

Colin leaned over and whispered,

"You are a vision tonight, beautiful."

Maggie turned her head and smiled. Colin was dressed in a suit and looked very debonair.

"You look nice yourself Collin."

Colin laughed,

"What this ole thing."

He handed me a glass of champagne and clinked his glass to mine.

"here's to a magical evening."

I lifted my glass,

"Yes, to a very magical evening."

"May I have this dance beautiful?"

"I thought you would never ask."

Collin took her glass and set both of their glasses on a table. He took her hand and led her to the dance floor. The band was playing a slow love song about a couple finally finding each other. Colin pulled Maggie in close, and they gently swayed to the music as they gazed into each other's eyes. To anyone watching it was just a simple dance involving two people. But to Maggie and Colin it was romantic. Colin whispered the words of the song in Maggie's ear. Maggie closed her eyes and leaned into Colin as he sang. As the song came to an end they reluctantly drew apart. They both clapped for the band.

Colin led her to their table. One of the waiters came by with glasses of champagne. Allison and Joshua came up to the table and Allison took a seat by Maggie.

"Mama this is great. Are you enjoying yourself? Are you going to dance?"

Collin signaled the waiter for two more glasses of champagne. Colin handed Allison a glass and said,

"Would it be ok to ask your mom to dance." Allison took a sip of champagne,

"I believe she said she was saving a dance for you."

Maggie hid her smile behind her glass as she shipped her champagne. Apparently, they had not been seen dancing already. Benjamin and Brittany walked up to the table and took the other two seats. Benjamin nodded hello to Colin and said,

"Mama you look too pretty to sit at the table all night. You should be dancing."

The band had started another slow song. Colin stood up and said,

"Excuse us but I think this is our dance."

He held out his hand to Maggie and led her out to the dance floor.

As the hours went by Maggie had danced a couple dozen times with Colin. At one point in the evening the band played a country song and the girls pulled Maggie out to the dance floor to dance a line dance.

Colin and the boys sat this dance out but watched as the ladies laughed and danced. The champagne flowed freely all evening . At one point in the evening the couples had stopped to eat.

At 11:55 the band made the announcement for everyone to grab a partner and hit the dance floor for the countdown. Maggie accepted Colins hand, and both walked out to the dance floor. When the music stopped the countdown began,

ten… nine….eight.

Everyone was loudly counting. Colin glanced around the area for Maggie's children. When he did not see them anywhere near, he pulled Maggie out the French doors to a secluded place away from prying eyes. The countdown continued,

three…two…one…

Colin took Maggie face in his hands and pulled her lips to his . As Maggie placed her hands on Collins's chest, he deepened the kiss. They could hear the partygoers yelling "Happy New Year" as the band played Auld Lang Syne.

Whistles and popping balloons could be heard but Maggie and Colin stayed glued to one spot neither wanting the kiss to end.

Chapter Fifteen

Six Weeks Later

The kids had been back in Alabama for six weeks. I facetimed with them as often as our schedules allowed. Colin and I had been almost inseparable since the minute the kids drove out of the apartment complex on their way to the airport.

We had lunch twice a week and dinner three times a week. Mostly I cooked and we would sit on the sofa necking as the kids called it. Every weekend we spent every waking hour together.

The first three weekends after the kids left, we spent out at his friend Wyatt's ranch. Those were wonderful fun filled days. We went horseback riding and four wheeling. At night we sat out by the firepit star gazing and stealing kisses, when, of course, no one was looking. This quickly became my favorite part of the weekend.

Betty, Wyatt's wife, and I had become fast friends. Several times she had drove into San Antonio and we would meet up for lunch, shopping or just having a spa afternoon.

The last three weeks Colin had been out of the country for his job. I was not sure where he was as it was on a need-to-know basis, but he texted me often and we were able to FaceTime every night. The time difference was tricky, but Colin always made it work. This was Valentine's weekend and Colin was coming home today. He had texted me a couple days ago and asked if I would like to go down to the coast for the weekend. We would be staying at his beach house, with separate rooms of course. Always a gentleman my sweet Colin was.

He was due home anytime and I was packed and ready. He told me to pack everything I would need in a backpack only . He said our mode of transportation was a surprise and I was to dress warmly for the trip. This had my curiosity going crazy.

I dressed in jeans, T shirt, and knee hi boots. I added a leather jacket that matched my boots. I loved the buttery feel of the Maroon colored leather.

I packed extra underwear and two shirts as well as a pair of walking shorts. I added a comfortable pair of sandals and a bathing suit just in case. Also, I added my hairbrush and my makeup bag as well as a decent pair of pajamas with a thin robe. I was uncertain if it would all fit in the backpack, but as I carefully rolled each item and layered them in the bag, I discovered I had plenty of room. So, I grab my tablet and chargers for both tablet and my cell phone. I was finally ready.

I already changed my purse to a small over the shoulder bag just big enough for my wallet and cell phone. I sipped on a glass of sweet tea and scrolled through my media pages as I waited for Colin to call.

I had a Valentine gift for Colin but as we would be in Corpus Christi tomorrow, he would have to wait till we came back on Sunday for the gift. I had made him a quilt. It was not a large quilt. Just a bit smaller than a twin size. It was good for a cover on the couch during cold weather. The material was blue with Air Force emblems. There was a flag in the bottom left corner. I added a small square on the right bottom corner that said,

Thank you for your service. Made by your 'Bama Girl.'

Our first weekend we had spent at the ranch his friend Wyatt referred to me as his Bama Girl. It made Colin smile.

I always tried to personalize every quilt I made. Especially if I was giving them as gifts. I lost count years ago and how many quilts I had made over my lifetime. Some sold but mostly I gifted.

My cell went off at that moment. It was a Text from Colin. It said if I were ready would I mind meeting him in the parking lot. I texted back that I was on my way down. I added a flashing heart emoji. I rinsed out my tea glass, set my alarm to the apartment, grabbed my backpack, and walked out the door.

In the parking lot I looked for Colin by his truck. He wasn't there. Confused I looked all around and at that moment I heard the loud rumble of a Harley motorcycle. It stopped right behind Colin's truck.

Colin climbed off the bike and removed his helmet. I quickly rushed to him, and he grabbed me in a tight hug. We stood there kissing and hugging for a bit. In between kisses he whispered in my ear how much he had missed me and this as he kissed me again.

When we finally broke apart, he asked if my adventurous side was ready to go. I looked over at his beautiful bike that I knew absolutely nothing about and said,

"We are riding on that?"

" Yes, unless you rather not".

"Oh no, I rather, trust me I rather. No wonder I had to pack a backpack. You are always so full of surprises. This is going to be so much fun. Let's go" .

He walked over to his truck an unlocked the door and reached inside for a helmet. He placed it on my head and fastened it down. While he continued to adjust the straps, he explained to me how there were speakers and a microphone in the helmet so we could talk along the way or just listen to the music.

He took my backpack and put it inside one of the saddle bags on the side of the bike. He pulled my face shield down but first he kissed me again. He climbed on the bike, and I gingerly climbed on behind him. I pulled my purse strap, so the bag was in front of me . He reached back and pulled my arms around his waist.

"Are you comfortable enough."

With excitement in my voice I said, "yes, let's go".

He leaned the bike to displace the kickstand and I yelped out and grabbed his jacket tightly with my fingers. He reached back and patted my thigh. He started the engine. As the bike roared to life, I hugged him tighter. Once again, he reached back and patted my thigh. He had a 60's music station playing, but when he spoke the music would fade away.

"Here we go babe."

The ride to Corpus was the most exciting ride of my life. The vibration of the engine. The wind swirling around us. Riding on a bike brought everything near quickly. As the scenery blurred by, the warm sun felt wonderful. I snuggled closer to him and tighten my arms around him. Occasionally he would stroke my thigh.

Often, I would see something that excited me, and I would say " Did you see that?"

He would pat my thigh again and laughingly say "I'm driving babe".

Chapter Sixteen

We arrived in Corpus in just over two hours. Colin pulled into the parking lot of a barbecue stand. There was a sign that said,

"Best BBQ in Town".

Colin turned the engine off and said to me, "You climb off first, Maggie."

I was cautious as to how I would be able to swing my leg over. I was not sure if I could even stand. My whole body was still vibrating. I finally found my legs and Colin was able to climb off. He removed his helmet and hung it on his bike. He reached over to take mine off. I shook my hair out and he placed my helmet on the bike too.

He reached for my hand and leaned in to kiss me. "You, ok?"

"Yes, my legs are a little shaky, but I loved every second of the ride."

We walked up to the counter and Colin spoke in Spanish to the owner of the barbecue stand. They shook hands and from what little Spanish I knew I deduced they were friends. Colin ordered our food and drinks then we walked over to a table near the bike .

"I ordered us both Carne Guisada tacos and sweet tea. I hope that was OK. I thought we should eat before heading out to the beach house."

"That was a great idea Colin, and yes tacos will be simply fine. I take it from what little Spanish I have picked up over the last few months that the owner is a friend?"

"Yes. Mateo and his wife Rosaria have eight children. They came to America thirty years ago. They were migrant farm workers. At the end of the season the couple who owned the farm took them in. At the time Rosaria was pregnant with their first child. She was unable to travel back to Mexico. The family helped them by getting them extended work permits They also helped both to become legal citizens.

The couple became godparents to the first five children. They died about fifteen years ago. They left all they own to the five children and any future children who would come later. They also left Mateo and Rosaria $25,000.

They took the money and opened this barbecue place. They still live in the home the couple left them. Legally it belongs to the eight children, but it is all family.

All eight children were able to attend good schools and attend college from the generosity of that couple. It is an amazing story so much, so they were featured once on a TV show for food where they find all the best places in Texas to eat. They were honored with the best barbecue in town award. They could retire and live comfortable, but they love doing what they do .

They also have *paid it forward* by giving other families from Mexico the chance to come here work and become legal citizens. It was what the deceased couple always believed in."

 A young girl arrived at that moment with their food. They thanked her and she left to deliver other tables their food.

"That was an amazing story, Colin. I just fell in love with this place."

"In love huh?"

I smiled I knew my face was as red as my jacket. We had not said the L word yet. Colin laughed and we ate our food in mostly silence.
When we finished our tacos, Rosaria appeared with deep fried ice cream. She spoke to Colin in Spanish then turned to me and we talked in English for a few minutes.

I had taken a bite of ice cream and moaned. I told her it was to die for. She thanked me and said please come back again soon. We finished up our dessert and loaded back onto the bike.

We headed toward the Gulf. It was so beautiful it was only just after three in the afternoon. The sun was still shining bright . Fifteen minutes later Colin pulled into a cute cottage driveway. From the outside it looked small. Painted white with a blue trim. There were wooden shutters on all the windows. A white picket fence around a small front yard. There were beautiful shrubs and trees everywhere.

Colin clicked a button and a door opened. He drove the bike inside a small garage. He waited for me to get off then he climbed off too. We put our helmets on a shelf along the wall. He retrieved our bags from the saddlebags on the bike.

"The manager already came by and stocked the pantry and the fridge. I sent her a list of what I thought we could use. Are you ready for the grand tour."

"Oh yes, more than ready. This is a beautiful place."

Colin opened the door from the garage to a dainty kitchen. I oohed and awed as we walked through the cottage. Everything was decorated in Navy Blues, Reds, and Whites.

The kitchen was designed in a galley style. There was a gas stove, a French door fridge, and a dishwasher. Beautiful granite countertops and a lower counter with bar stools. It was an open concept kitchen and living room.

A small four chair table stood in a nook near the back French doors.

The living room furniture looked pleasing and comfortable. There was a widescreen TV on the wall that was accessible from the dining table as well as the kitchen.

We walked down the hall. A door to the right opened to good sized bedroom with an attached en-suite bathroom. The door to the left was a smaller bedroom but also had an en- suite bathroom.

Colin put his bag in the small room and mine in the big room. He took my hand and led me to the French doors. They opened to a large, covered patio.

A barbecue area was built to one side . A sitting area with a fire pit was on the other side. There was table with chairs and overhead fans. Beautiful potted plants were arranged in several places. I noticed a walking trail that went down the back through the trees. I asked Colin where it led to. He still had a hold of my hand and as he pulled me to his side, we walked down the path.

Just after we cleared the trees miles and miles of beautiful sand met us. And just beyond the sand was the Gulf. I clapped my hand in Glee. Like a kid in a candy store.

There was a bench to one side of the walkway. Colin and I sat down and pulled our boots off. I took my jacket off and rolled my jeans up as high as I could. Taking Collins hand, we ran down the Sandy beach to the water's edge.

Wave after wave lapped at our feet . We would run in and out again laughing as the waves always tried to beat us. This went on for a while then we strolled along the beach arm and arm.

There were only a few people on the beach. Collin's cabin was one of about twenty along that stretch of beach All were mostly air BNB's.

   "Are you tired? We could head back now if you like."

      "I'm not tired, but I do need to use the restroom."

         He laughed and pulling my arm said, "come on."

We arrived back at the cottage and Colin showed me an outdoor shower for rinsing the sand off. He rinsed off our feet and we went inside.

I excused myself and went to my assigned room. I used the bathroom and washed my face and hands.

I unpacked the clothes I had brought and hung them up. I changed out of my jeans into shorts . I regretted not bringing another pair of jeans. As I was brushing my hair, Colin knocked on the door.

"It's open, come in."

He opened the door and said, "I am throwing my jeans in the washer and wondered if you wanted to add yours."

" Yes, I do. I was just wishing I had brought another pair. These are wet with sand."

I walked into the bathroom and collected my jeans. Instead of handing them to Colin I reached for his instead. I had noticed a washer and dryer in the garage when we arrived.

"I'll just take these out to the garage."

Colin reluctantly handed me the basket with his clothes.

"I'll just pour us both a glass of wine and meet you out on the patio."

We sat out on the patio for a while and drank wine. Colin talked a little about his trip. I told him more about Betty's and my shopping trips. A few hours later we walked inside to prepare dinner.
We found an enchilada casserole in the fridge with a note saying,

"Heat at 400 degrees for 30 minutes, A salad is prepared in the green bowl. Enjoy. JJ."

Colin smiled,

"JJ is the manager of the AB&B and an excellent cook."

While the food was warming, we got out plates and silver ware and set the table. Colin opened another bottle of wine and left it to breathe. I found a radio and turned on a country music station out of San Antonio . I turned the volume down and Colin took my hand and we danced in the kitchen. I could feel his warm breath in my hair.

My heart was beating fast. I knew I was in love with this man, but I was too shy to say the words. The song changed several times, but we just stood there in the same spot swaying back and forth lost in our world.

Chapter Seventeen

Saturday morning arrived shining brightly. I had slept with the windows open so I could hear the ocean sounds as I slept. Now I heard the ocean as well as birds. The curtains were gently swaying in the breeze. I stretched and rolled over to look out the window. I should get up, but the bed was so comfy, and the warm breeze felt so good.
I smiled as I cuddle my pillow remembering the night before.

Colin and I had danced without moving our feet until the buzzer from the oven sounded alerting us the food was ready. We enjoyed our dinner of casserole and salad. After we cleaned up the kitchen, Colin grabbed the wine bottle and our glasses, and we went out to the patio. Colin lit the fire pit and we sat and talked for hours.

It seemed as if we were never at a loss for something to talk about. I had tried to hide my yawn, but Colin being the amazing gentleman he was, pulled me from my chair and walked me to my bedroom door.

He pulled me into his arms. Softly and slowly, he kissed me. I put my arms around his neck and pulled his head to my lips. I felt Collin's hands rubbing up and down my back. I seductively touched his lips with my tongue. He gently tugged at my tongue as the kiss deepened. The heat between us was undeniable. I am sure the wine played a big role in that; however, passion was never absent from our kisses.

Colin pulled away and reached over to open the bedroom door. He gently pushed me into the room kissed the tip of my nose and said,

"Sweet dreams, until tomorrow."

The smell of coffee and bacon brought me back from my ruminating. I threw the cover off and went to the bathroom. I washed my face and hands and brushed my teeth. I looked in the mirror. No makeup. Well, here was the mother of all tests. Let's see if he runs away after seeing the real me without makeup. I smiled; I knew he would not.
I pulled on my robe and padded barefoot out to the kitchen .

"Good morning beautiful."

Colin handed me a Cup of coffee with a quick kiss.

"Did you sleep ok?"

"Yes, I did, thank you for the coffee."

"I heard you up, so I got it ready for you."

Leaning in to kiss again him I whispered, "Always a perfect gentleman."

Kissing me back Colin said,

"Maybe not perfect, but with you always a gentleman." Wiggling his eyebrows up and down he continued talking. "No matter how hard it is."

We laughed and he turned back to the stove to finish making breakfast. I got the plates and silverware out of the cabinet. I found butter and jam as well as orange juice in the fridge. I placed everything on the countertop. We sat down at the bar and enjoyed the delicious breakfast.

" So, what are our plans for the day? Did you need to come down here to check on something?"

"No, I didn't have to come, but I wanted to bring you down. Happy Valentine's Day beautiful."

He got up and reached into cupboard. When he turned around, he handed me a bouquet of flowers.

"Only for you my Bama Girl."

"Oh Colin, they are so beautiful. Thank you so much."

I pulled out my cell phone and took a pic of them.

"We won't be able to take these back to San Antonio, so I'll enjoy them here and have a pic to look at later."

Laughing Colin said, "there will always be more Flowers for my beautiful Bama Girl."

We kissed and he just held me for a long time.

We spent the day on the bike. Colin took me on a wonderful excursion from Padre Island to Port Aransas. We rode down Mustang Island stopping occasionally to take pics. We stopped for lunch at a seafood spot on the beach.

After lunch we drove to the pier and walked the entire length. It was a bit windy out on the Gulf, but I enjoyed it so much. Early in the afternoon we headed back to Colin's cottage.

I went to my room to shower and change while Colin threw some steaks on the grill. When I joined him on the patio, he had a chilled bottle of champagne and a bowl of chocolate covered strawberries waiting for me. He placed a strawberry to my lips, and I took a bite. The juice ran down my chin and Colin leaned and kissed the juice away. He handed me a glass of champagne and we toasted to a beautiful day.

Colin slipped inside to shower. I finished up the side dishes of salad and baked potatoes. I set the patio table. Everything was ready to eat when he walked back out.

Colin returned and he reached for me. He kissed me soft and sweetly. He handed me a single rose and a beautifully wrapped box and whispered, "Happy Valentine's Day beautiful."

Opening the box, my hands were shaking from sheer happiness. The paper and ribbon fell to the floor. In the box was a beautiful Sterling Silver barrel clasp chain bracelet . He had loaded it with several charms.

Colin took the box from me and remove the bracelet. Taking my right arm, he fastened the bracelet on my wrist. After he was sure the clasp was securely locked, he turned the bracelet around on my wrist and said.

   "This charm represents your old life in Alabama." It was a charm of Alabama.

"This charm celebrates your new life in Texas." It was a charm of Texas.

"This charm is called Family Tree. It is to honor your wonderful family.

And this one here, is called interlocking hearts. It is yours and mine beating as one.

And this one, the last one for now and there will be more in the future, is called The Round Ball of Love. It signifies a never-ending love".

Tears were streaming down my face. Colin lifted my chin and gazed into my eyes. With his thumb he wiped at my tears and said,

"Maggie, I love you. From the moment you slipped and fell into my arms I felt a strong current run through my body. From that day on you are all I think about. I have never allowed myself to feel this way for any woman in my entire life. I have always been a career man. I have devoted my life to the Air Force, but lady you have totally rocked my world. I love you. I never want to be without you. This bracelet is the beginning of a courtship for us. It means telling your children and our friends we are embarking on a journey together. I am not asking you to marry me today but make no mistake I do intend to ask you. Now dry your tears and kiss me."
I kissed him with all the passion I could implore on him. When we broke apart, I said,

"I love you. I have known for a long time. Colin, never have I ever felt this kind of love. Thank you for loving me too"!

He kissed me again and said, "foods getting cold let's eat."

We left Padre Island the next day around noon. We arrived back in San Antonio around 4:00 in the afternoon. It took longer going back because we stopped at several places along the way to take pictures. Back at the apartment, Colin parked his bike in one of the garages available for residents. He carried our bags and held my hand as we walked up to my apartment. I put on a pot of coffee and Colin order us dinner. After dinner we sat on the couch holding hands and watching TV. It was late when Colin kissed me goodnight. It was a marvelous feeling to finally say I love you as he left.

Chapter Eighteen

It has been several weeks since that wonderful Valentine's Day weekend. The weather in Texas was beginning to get colder. The weatherman was predicting snow. I was excited about the prospect of snow falling outside my windows. It was the only thing I missed about wintertime in Alabama.

Since returning home from Corpus, Colin and I had been inseparable. Well as inseparable as we could be. Every morning before work he would come up for coffee and whatever we were having for breakfast. He would then walk me to my car kiss me goodbye and tell me to drive safe.

Some days he showed up at my job and took me out to lunch. I always got home hours before he did. I would cook supper and when he came home, he would stop at his apartment to shower and change out of his uniform. He would then come up stairs to eat. We always washed-up supper dishes together.

After supper we would sit on the couch and watch our favorite shows. After the news went off, he would reluctantly go home. Our goodnight kisses were growing stronger and more passionate.

The only night during the week he did not stay after supper was his poker night with his friends. I spent those nights in my sewing room. Even then he always came up for our goodnight kisses.

I was falling more and more in love with him every day. He was smart, direct, full of integrity and self-confident. Colin always had a positive attitude. And his smile… ummm when he smiled at me and his eyes lit up, I just wanted to swoon.

I love the way he respected my opinions and always listen to me. If I need his opinion, he will give it but only if I ask. I found it impossible to argue with him. He had so much charisma. He oozed charm and sophistication. And passion, oh he was so passionate. I wanted more of him, but he respected me enough not to push for more than our kisses.

I had stopped comparing Colin to Gregory. There was no comparison. Missy was right. Gregory was not a normal man.

There is no way he was ever in love with me. He loved the idea that I belong to him. He loved controlling me. I thank God every night for allowing me to find a man like Colin. A real Genuine man with morals.

I wrapped a blanket around me and stepped out onto the patio. The wind was chilly, and I could feel ice in the air. I took several deep breaths of air and slowly released them. I looked up at the dark clouds. Yes, we were most definitely going to get some snow. Excitement ran through me, and I stepped back into the apartment.

I turned on my electric fireplace and told Alexa to play an oldies station.

I had made a huge pot of chili and a pan of cornbread for our supper tonight. It was perfect winter weather comfort food. I had made a big pot so Colin could take the leftovers to his apartment for his buddies to eat during their poker game.

After supper tonight Colin would leave and go back down to his apartment for poker with his buddies. I had planned on a FaceTime with Allison.

It will be the first time that I tell her about Colin and me. I keep putting it off for fear of her rejection of him. I did not want her negativity to spill onto what I have with him.

I glanced at the Clock. Colin was home and would be up at any time. We had exchanged codes to both of our door locks. That way we did not have to knock.

I set the table. I had separate bowls of diced green onions, grated cheese, and sour cream waiting as toppings for the chili. The cornbread was sliced and arranged on a plate. The chili was simmering on the stove to keep warm.

I fixed us both a glass of sweet tea. I had made an Apple pie and it was warming in my warmer. It would be delicious with ice cream for dessert later after Colin came back up from his poker night.

I heard the beeping of the door lock. I walked out of the kitchen right into Colin's arms. His kisses were always delightful and the best part of my day. I loved kissing, but what really got me was how he would just hold me tight and lovingly caressed my back.

I knew he was smelling my hair. He would bury his face in my neck and lovingly sniff my hair. He would nibble on my neck or my earlobe.

Kissing me he murmured against my lips, "mmmmm smells good".

"I made chili and cornbread."

"Yes, it smells delicious, but I meant you. You smell good."

I laughed and lovingly swatted his arm, "you are so funny must be why I love you so darn much."

"Baby, I love your smell, your laugh, your dainty little toes. And your hair, I love the way it shimmers and shines and softly falls through my fingers. You are beautiful. I am in love with you baby."

I kissed him again and took him by the hand and led him to the kitchen table . I ladled out several scoops of chili into a bowl and placed it on his plate. I only got one scoop for myself.

"Be careful it's hot. I made extra for your poker night."

"The guys are going to love that. We will not be playing long the weather is expected to turn for the worse. Wyatt already texted he will not be able to make it. They get the bad weather before we do."

"I'm going to FaceTime with Allison later. It is time I tell her about us."

"How do you feel about that baby?"

"I'm OK I think." I laughed 'It is time to fess up."

"It will be OK baby; you have good kids. They love you and will be happy you are happy."

Later, after we finished with supper, I helped Colin carry all the food downstairs to his apartment. Gary and Todd were just arriving and helped to open the door and carry things in. After we set everything down in his kitchen, Colin walked me back upstairs to my apartment.

I kissed him and told him to enjoy his night. As always, he reluctantly turned and left.

Chapter Nineteen

I walked into my apartment and made a cup of hot tea. Taking my tea and Getting my Tablet I climbed into my comfortable chair and called Allison.

I took a sip of tea just as Allison answered. "Hi mama."

"Hello my baby girl." I could hear the kids in the background.

"Do you have company?"

"No ma'am, Ben, Brittany and the kids are here. Ben is helping Josh out in the garage. So, Brittany is here too".

Brittany's face appeared in view "Hi mom."

"I'm glad you're both there. Do you two have time for a quick chat?"

"Sure mama, the boys are watching a cartoon and the girls are bugging them."

"Well, I bet that's fun to watch". I laughed. "So, girls, I have some news."

"Oh, we heard on the news you might be getting snow."

"Yes Allison, we are supposed to, but that's not my news."

Both girls looked at each other and then looked back at me.

"What's up mama?"

"You girls remember Colin? From New Year's Eve?"

"Yes, what about him Mama?" Allison asked skeptically.

"We have been dating. A lot. Like every day."

"What! Mama really?" Allison shrieked!

"That's wonderful mom, Benjamin and I we're just talking about how we hoped you were getting out and doing things and we both like Colin. He's a great looking sexy man for an old man." Brittney laughed.

"Brittney really." Allison turned from Brittany back to the screen "mama what do you mean dating every day?"

"Just that. We spend every hour we're not working or sleeping," sleeping said loudly. "together"

" Mama, are you having sex with him?" Allison said with a shaky voice.

"Allison!" Britney admonished to Allison, "you cannot ask your mother that kind of question. That's not a mother daughter question."

Turning to me propping her face on her hand Brittany said, "but I can ask, are you? Is he good? I bet he is. Do you use protection?"

"Oh my God mama! What if you get pregnant?" Allison whined.

I just sat back and sipped my tea while both girls went on and on. I would smile and nod and sip my tea some more. Finally, both girls stopped talking and as if they remembered I was still on FaceTime with them, turned and looked at me.

"Are y'all finished? Can I speak now?

Both girls said "yes ma'am" at the same time.

"Well, too many questions. Let's see if I can answer them all.
First, I had dated Colin a couple times before y'all were here for Christmas."

Allison started to speak but one look from me and she closed her mouth.

"Remember the video I sent the boys of the parade?"

Both girls shook their heads yes.

"Well, that was our first date. Then we had a couple more. Oh, and he also drove me to Fredericksburg to buy my Christmas tree. He has also had supper with me here in my apartment.
He took me out to his friends ranch one weekend. We rode horses. Cooked out. Had F.U.N.

After y'all left to go back home, we picked back up. We kept it secret from you. He respected me enough to not interfere with our visit.

Since New Year's Eve we discovered we liked each other tremendously. Colin has never married. The Air Force was his only love.
This past Valentine's Day we rode his Harley,"

At the word Harley both girls gasped but kept quiet,

"Down to Corpus Christi. He owns a beautiful beach cottage there and we spent the weekend."

I raised my eyebrows as a warning not to speak.

"We had a marvelous time he gave me this charm bracelet." I held my arm up and turned my wrist back and forth letting the charms Jingle.

"He told me he loved me. Not just loved me but was head over heels IN love with me. I told him I loved him too.
And I do girls, so very much. I have never been this happy in my entire life except for raising my two beautiful children.

Now for your most private question. No, we are not having sex. He has amazing respect for me . As for me getting pregnant, Allison," I stared right into her eyes,

"Your father made me get my tubes tied after you were born. He did not want any more kids."

Tears fell from Allison's eyes. Brittany leaned over to her and hugged her .

Sniffling Allison said "I'm so sorry mama I didn't know. Ben I both know daddy was mean to you. We never actually saw it, but we always knew mama . If Colin makes you happy then I am happy. That is all we have ever wanted for you. Is to be safe and happy."

Brittney chimed in, "I'm so glad you're finally admitting it to us. I sort of had the idea something more was going on when we were there for Christmas. I even told Ben. He said he sure hoped so because he really likes Colin."

"We all do mama." Allison said "And Mama you are so beautiful. You have a glow about you."

"OK before y'all get me started crying, go get my babies so I can chat with them."

I spent the next thirty minutes laughing and chatting with the four children. The girls kept kissing the screen giving me kisses. The boys talked about anything and everything.

After we signed off, I sat there for a while and let the previous conversation overcome me. That is where Colin found me later, when he let himself into my apartment.

Chapter Twenty

Colin was going out of town again. He averaged one to two weeks every month to travel to different Air Force bases. We had discussed him retiring, but I think he genuinely loves the Air Force and does not want to retire. I never want to be the reason he does retire from the Air Force.

We were going out to dinner tonight and I was dressed and ready. We had found a street cafe that served Cajun food. We both love the atmosphere and the food. We had gotten to know the owner and was on a first-name basis with him . We had our own table we enjoyed sitting at. It was small and cozy and overlooked Interstate 410. I was dressed in jeans and a sweater with boots.

Colin came in and saw me standing out on the balcony. It was my favorite place to be. The snow we had a few weeks earlier lasted all of one day. Then the weather went back to the mid-70s. It was always a little cooler at night though .

Colin slipped in behind me and wrapped his arms around me. The heat from his body immediately sent ways of euphoria through me. I could smell his aftershave and it was intoxicating. I leaned back into him and wrapped my arms over his. He nibbled on my neck and nipped at my ear, causing more waves of euphoria.

"What's going on in that pretty head of yours?"

"Just watching the Sky, it's so beautiful when the sun is setting."

"I could stand here all night and hold you but I'm hungry. Are you ready to go?"

"Yes dear, let me grab my purse."

"Not until you give me this..."

He turned me to face him, and his lips met mine. The kiss was soft at first. He tasted of mint, and I suddenly wanted more. I touched his lips with the tip of my tongue. He opened his mouth and hungrily deepened the kiss. He pulled me tighter to him. I pulled his head harder to my lips. We were hungry for each other.

I did not want to stop the kiss. I wanted more. I wanted him to carry me to the bed and make love to me. I needed him and I knew he wanted me to. He suddenly pulled back and rested his forehead on mine . He took several deep breaths and said,

"Baby we have to stop. I do not want to, but if you keep kissing me that way, I will not be able to control myself. Baby I love you. I want to make love to you. But I want our first time to be in a marriage bed."

"I know honey it's just you tasted so good, and my desire took control. Let's go to supper."

Colin took my hand, and we walk to my car. Colin was having his truck serviced and it was to chilly ride the Harley. I got in on the passenger side. He leaned in for one more kiss. My hand on his cheek I smiled at him seductively.

"Lady you're killing me." He groaned.

I laughed and he closed my door.

At the cafe we were met by our favorite waitress. Jenny was a young mother of two. Her husband was in the Navy and was deployed.

She lived with her parents who helped with the children so she could work. Normally we would have been seated by a hostess, but Jenny saw us walking in, so she grabbed the menus and led us to our special table.

"How are you two tonight?"

"We are hungry Jenny."

Jenny laughed at Colins joke and said, "You want your usual drinks?"

"Yes, Jenny and thank you." Colin said.

Jenny left to go get our drinks while Colin and I perused the menu.

"Think I will have the catfish plate with fries, slaw and hush puppies. Do you know what you want?"

I looked over the seafood section and decided to try something different. "I think I'll have the jambalaya with cornbread."

We had decided on our choice, so Colin placed the menus to the side. He reached over for my hand and kissed my knuckles.

We stared at each other. His breath on my hand sending shivers over me.

Jenny arrived with our drinks and Colin told her what we were having.

"OK folks I'll go place this order. Can I get you anything else?"

"No thank you dear we're fine." I looked over at Colin and he shook his head yes to let her know he agreed with me.

Colin continued to hold my hand as he spoke, "my next trip is coming up I'll be gone a week this time."

"Am I allowed to know where you're going this time?"

"Sure, I'll be at Arnold in Tennessee."

"Really that is just a short drive from my hometown."

"Well, if you weren't working, I could take you with me."

" I didn't know you could do that."

"Yes, I just have to add your name to the flight plan."

"Well, sadly I can't go. I love my job too much to take a chance on losing it."

"There will be more trips in the future. We will go everywhere when the time is right."

"I love you, Colin."

"I love you too baby."

We talked a little more before Jenny showed up with our food. We ate and chatted about what I had planned to do while he was gone. After we finished our supper, we ordered a bread pudding with ice cream for dessert. Jenny brought us coffee and told us the owner would be by to chat.

Pops, the owner came over and pulled out a chair after shaking Colins hand and patting my shoulder. He asked if the food was OK tonight. I told him my jambalaya was extremely delicious and it had just the right taste of spices. Pops said he was glad we enjoyed our meal. Colin and Pops carried on a conversation for about fifteen minutes when someone came by and said Pops was needed.

He stood up and said "thanks for coming by tonight folk's bye" we said goodbye and Colin motion to Jenny for the ticket. He handed her his credit card to pay for our meal. She returned quickly and handed it to Colin. He filled out the tip and signed his name. Colin was very generous. He always gave Jenny a twenty-dollar tip. Which was almost fifty percent of the ticket instead of the normal twenty percent. We got up to leave and Jenny gave me a hug and turned to Colin and said, "thank you and have a good rest of your night."

We left the cafe and Colin asked if I would like to see a movie. I said yes and we drove to the cinema. A new fantasy movie was out, and we both had expressed how we would like to see it.

After we found our seats, Colin put his arm around me, and I snuggled into him. The night was perfect. And I knew it would be another great memory.

Chapter Twenty-One
Colin

It was getting harder and harder to take these trips for work. I hated every minute spent without Maggie. I had been talking to her about putting in for my retirement. The Air Force is the only life I have ever known. Maggie was quickly replacing that space in my heart. She was always on my mind. Wyatt told me I was in crazy love. Betty called it smitten. Whatever it is I know that I love her, and I want to spend the rest of my life with her.

I had a surprise for her. She knows I am headed to Arnold Air Force Base in Tennessee. What she does not know is I am planning to talk to her son Benjamin. I wanted to speak to him about asking his mother to marry me. I was not asking for permission as much as making sure he and his sister would be ok with the idea. I hoped he will accept the fact that I am going to ask her with or without their approval. But I did not want to be the cause of any hard feelings with her children. She had great kids and I was hoping to be a pop-pop to the grandchildren. They were sweet children and my only chance at being a grandfather.

My work here at Arnold will be finished up as of today . I rented a car for the drive one hundred and ten miles south through Alabama. I checked the GPS, and it is about a two-hour drive. My plan is to wait until I arrive in her hometown to contact her son.

The drive down to Alabama was beautiful. No wonder Maggie missed it so much. If I could get her to retire early, I would buy a home here. I can live anywhere that she is. It would make her happy to be around her family again.

I had checked into the hotel and my call to Benjamin could not be put off any longer, so I dialed his number.

 "Hello."

" Hello Benjamin?"

 "Yes, this is he."

 "This is Colin, your mom's friend."

 "Yes, how are you doing Colin? Is mama, ok?"

"Yes, yes she is fine. I would like to talk to you if you have the time."

"Sure, I have the time what's up?"

"Not on the phone. I'm in town. Is there somewhere we could meet?"

"Yes, where are you?"

"I'm at the Holiday Inn just off the Interstate."

"Oh ok, well I can meet you there or you wanna grab a beer?"

"Where can we meet?" Benjamin gave me directions to a local bar, and I drove over to it. I was waiting inside when Benjamin walked in. I motioned him over and told the waitress to bring us a couple beers on tap. He walked up to the table, and I stood to shake his hand.

"Does mama know you're here Colin?

"No no she doesn't. Let's get our beer and I'll explain while I'm here."

The waitress brought our mugs of beer and set them down in front of us. We both took a hefty drink.

"That's good beer. This place looks new."

"Yes, we were a dry county up until about two years ago. This is the only bar in this town."

"Wow! Really? I didn't know they still had dry counties."

"Yes, it took a while to finally get it voted in. This area is mostly Bible Belt. But with the new generation coming up it is starting to change in some areas. A beer every now and then never hurt." Ben said laughing.

"Well, I guess I will get down to why I'm here."

Benjamin listened attentively.

"Benjamin, I know you know your mother and I have been seeing each other."

"Yes Sir. Personally, I was glad to hear it. Allison wasn't at first, but she just wants mama to be safe and happy. We both have saw a huge change in her. She is so happy. Smiling and laughing more than we ever remember in all our lives."

"Your mother is an incredibly special lady. I have never married. I made the Air Force my life, but your mother has made a big change in that life. I want you to know I have the utmost respect for her. I have never nor would I ever do anything immoral or disrespectful where your mother is concerned."

"Thank you, Sir, I appreciate your honesty in that."

"Please call me Colin. Sir is reserved for the enlisted men and women." Colin smiled.

"OK Colin. So can I guess at why you're here without mama?"

Colin shook his head yes.

"You want to marry her, don't you?"

"Yes, I do. And just to be clear I am not here to ask permission, but to let you and your sister know it is important to your mother that I have your approval."

"Well Colin, we are more than happy to have you join our family. Let's go tell the brood. I'll text Brittany to meet us at Allison's and to let Allison know I'm on my way over. I take it we're not to inform Mama of this visit?"

"Yes, please let me be the one to tell her."

I followed Benjamin to Allison's home where I was welcomed with open arms. We planned for them to all FaceTime with us the moment that I proposed. Now to fly home and plan a very romantic outing.

Chapter Twenty-Two

The Proposal

Colin was home and we were getting ready to go out to supper. He advised me to dress to the nines . I took this to mean to fancy up, so I went by the mall on my way home from work and bought a new dress. It was emerald green with a V cut neckline and A-line skirt. It had three quarter sleeves. I decided to put my hair up in a stylish bun with the little curls pulled out. My pearls went nice with the dress, and I wore black strap heels. I grabbed a small black clutch to carry my cell phone and wallet.

I was just finishing putting on my shoes when Colin walked in.

"Oh yeah there is my beautiful Bama girl. You look amazing but then you always do."

"Thank you, my love. You look very dapper yourself. Where are we going tonight?"

"All I'm telling you is it's downtown. Now my lady our chariot awaits us."

"Our chariot? Humm curious as all get out here Colin."

Colin kissed me to stop me talking and led me out of the apartment to the elevator. As we stepped outside to the parking lot a long white limo was waiting. I gasped in surprise . "Colin, a limo?"

"Shhh no questions please my love." He turned to the driver and said "thank you. You have the info?"

"Yes Sir."

He closed the door after Colin was sitting inside. Colin put his arm around me and pulled me tightly to him. He took my hand and nibbled on my fingers.

"Why the secrets Colin? What are you planning?"

"I'm planning a romantic dinner with my girl. The limos for show and I want to snuggle with you instead of driving. Also, parking is difficult on a Friday night downtown."

"OK my love this is your show. I'll let you run it, but it will cost you."

"Oh yeah"

"Oh yeah. Now kiss me."

We kissed and snuggled all the way downtown. The limo driver dropped us off at the downtown Marriott. Colin took my arm and we walked inside. We were immediately directed to the elevator which took us to the rooftop. My eyes widen and I raised an eyebrow at Colin. He kissed the fingers of my left my hand he was holding and whispered, "Shhhh."

I smiled at him and shook my head no and clicked my tongue. Colin laughed out loud and hugged me to him.

"Almost sweetheart."

The door opened an immediately I saw a table decorated. There were small twinkling lights and soft music playing. Colin led me to the table and held my chair out for me. The waiter poured us both a glass of chilled champagne and told Colin our food would be out shortly.

I oohed and awed over all the beautiful decorations. Colin filled me in on the history of this rooftop. He told me some funny stories and I laughed.

Our food arrived and we enjoyed our dinner. After we finished with dinner the waiter suddenly appeared to remove the dishes and brought dessert. Baked Alaska Flambe. When the waiter caught it on fire, I jumped and clapped my hands giggling. Colin laughed at my antics.

The night could not have been more romantic and beautiful. Colin fed me a bite of the Baked Alaskan and it melted divinely in my mouth. I licked my lips as he leaned in and kissed me. He alternated feeding us both but with every bite he fed me he leaned in and kissed me.

Soon the waiter came back and remove our dishes and refilled our campaign glasses. He disappeared quickly just as the music changed that was playing in the background . The song was slow and romantic, so Colin took my hand and led me out to the floor. We danced and he whispered in my ear how beautiful I looked and how much he loved me. I nibbled on his ear and his arms tightened around me.

When the song ended, he led me back to the table. There was a large screen tablet propped up on the table. I look at it and back at Colin. He motioned for me to sit. As I sat, he got down on one knee. I gasped and he took my hands.

"Maggie you are an amazing woman. You are beautiful, sweet, kind, sexy," he said wiggling his eyebrows up and down, "and a great mom. You have completely turned my life upside down I love you with every fiber of my being. I need you in my life. I want you in my life forever. Will you please be my wife?"

He opened a small box black box and a beautiful diamond ring sparkled with the lights. I could not speak. Tears were flowing down my cheeks. He removed the ring from the box and took my left hand,

"Will you marry me?"

I suddenly heard loud screaming, "say yes Mama!" Colin reached over and clicked the button on the tablet. All eight of my children were there on the screen. I glanced at the screen and then back at Colin.

"I… I Oh my gosh how did you?"

"Mama, answer the man he's waiting."

I look back at Colin and flung myself into his arms. He stood just in time to keep from falling backwards.

"Yes, yes a thousand times yes. I will marry you."

The kids were clapping and yelling as Colin slipped the ring on my finger. He then took me in his arms and kissed me passionately. The kids continued to yell and clap. I turned into screen with Colin behind me. He wrapped his arms around me I held out my hand. The diamond twinkled in the lights.

Allison was the first to speak. "Mama we are so incredibly happy for you. We know you are curious as to how and why we are all gathered to watch Colin propose, but it is a special night, so we are signing off. Colin, you fill her in. She's gonna have lots of questions."

Colin thanked them all for sharing the moment and among all the byes and throwing kisses he turned off the tablet. He held me again and kissed me.

" I know you have questions and I'll fill you in."

Colin spent the next fifteen minutes telling me about his trip and talking to Benjamin and Allison. He told me it was Britney's idea to FaceTime the moment that I proposed. I kissed him and thanked him for being him.

The waiter arrived and took the tablet, and we rode the elevator down and I saw that our limo was waiting we rode back to my apartment kissing the whole way.

Chapter Twenty-Three

"Mama you have to have a big wedding."

Allison was getting more excited about my wedding every time we FaceTime. I told her I just wanted something small, but she was wearing me down fast. Colin had proposed to me in April. He told me he wanted me to have the wedding of my dreams. He also said to not drag it out. So, we settled on a June wedding.

I planned as much as I could but working everyday left me only the evenings and weekends. Colin suggested I get a wedding planner. So, I gave in, and we interviewed several until we found the perfect lady. Her name was Marisol. And she was a fierce go-getter.

I tried to use the money in my 911 account to pay for the wedding, but Colin would not hear of it. I did insist on buying my own dress and my girls dresses. He gave in after I wore him down with kisses.

He gave Marisol a check for Twenty-Thousand dollars as a deposit.

She sent me a PDF of her list of questions. In the evenings Colin and I would go over the list answering as many questions as we could with available dates for meeting with various places.

Colin did not have any family left. He had asked Wyatt to be his best man. He had also asked Benjamin and Joshua to be his groomsmen. I had asked Allison and Brittany to be my bridesmaids. The baby girls, Sophia, and Olivia would be the flower girls and the boys, Benji and Logan, the ringbearers. I did not have many friends, so I asked Betty to be my maid of honor.

After giving Marisol our list of names with phone numbers and email addresses she sent everyone a To Do List.

We both wanted a French vanilla cake with lemon filling and buttercream icing. However, we were still scheduled for a cake testing in a week on a Friday evening. I asked for lots of daisies and baby's breath for Flowers. We had decided to get married on the rooftop of the downtown Marriott Hotel. The reception would follow in the same venue. Colin and I wanted June 19th as the day.

Marisol let us know she had reserved six rooms for three days. We chose to have the normal chicken or fish with vegetables as our meals but for our wedding rehearsal we were having Mexican food.

I talked to the girls on FaceTime every few days. Both girls were flying out to San Antonio to go dress shopping. Marisol said we were really pushing to have a dress on time, but I had every faith in her to get it done.

The girls arrived on a Saturday morning. Our appointments for trying on dresses was two hours after they arrived. They would only be here overnight. They had a return flight home on Sunday afternoon. Betty decided that we would have a girl's night out after we were through with dress shopping. Both girls were excited. Colin had generously given us the use of his house on the beach in Corpus Christi . He also ordered a limo to drive us down an another to drive us back.

I felt like a princess trying on different dresses but finally settled on a lite rose-pink design. I did not feel I could wear white, but I did go with a floor length dress. The girls both got rose gold t-length dresses and Betty went with a dark rose gold with a full-length skirt to color coordinate.

The Boys, Benjamin, and Joshua as well as Wyatt and Colin would wear black tuxedos with rose gold accents. Both little boys would also wear matching tuxedos with rose gold accents. The small pillows they would carry would be light pink, with darker gold strings to hold the rings. Both baby girls would wear light pink dresses with rose gold headbands. They would both carry pink baskets with pink roses to scatter.

My father had passed away years before and my mother lived with her sister. They both belonged to a travel group and were always going on a trip somewhere. But she had promised to be in San Antonio for my wedding. She had never met Colin, but they had FaceTime and she admired him greatly. I had decided I did not need anyone to give me away. I would walk to Colin alone.

The girls loved Corpus from the moment we arrived later that day. They both shared a room, and Betty I shared the big room. We spent most of the afternoon on the beach. Then Betty made us margaritas and we had tequila shots. The Manager of the BNB, JJ, came by with lots of finger foods for us to munch on. It was a lot of fun, but I missed Colin terribly.

The last time I was here was in February and I had a wonderful memory. Betty and I took the girls on a short trip around the island on Sunday morning and we had brunch near the pier. It was not long before the limo arrived, and we headed back to San Antonio and to the airport to drop off Allison and Brittany.

I text Colin to let him know we were back in San Antonio. Both he and Wyatt were at his apartment when Betty and I arrived. Both Wyatt and Betty laughed at how Colin and I kissed and whispered how we missed each other. Wyatt saying, we were like teenagers in our first love. Colin said I was his first love. I blushed because I knew both Betty and Wyatt knew I had been married before but not the conditions of my marriage. To me Colin was my first real love.

We four went out to dinner then Wyatt and Betty headed home. Colin and I headed to my apartment and my couch to catch up on missed hugs and lots of missed kisses.

Chapter Twenty-Four
The Wedding

To say I was nervous was putting it mildly. I was way beyond nerves. The only thing that calmed my nerves was knowing that at the end of this day I would be married to Colin.

My kids had arrived a couple days ago and last night we all stayed downtown at the Marriott.

Marisol, my wedding coordinator was running around everywhere making sure all was well, and everything was being done and on time.

Gary and Maria's twin granddaughters were helping with the children. Of course, both boys were with their dads getting dressed and acting all grown up. The twins were with the little girls.

The rehearsal dinner last night was so much fun. All the children had us laughing. When it was the little girls turn to walk down the aisle Sofia would throw one rose petal an Olivia would pick it up and put it in her basket.

We had to have the twins walk with them and show them how to throw the pedals and leave them on the ground. After four trips they finally got the idea of what to do. We told the twins to be on standby in case they were needed; Collin and I had given both girls $200 gift card to their favorite stores.

My mother and my aunt Lucille had arrived yesterday, and Maria had taken them both in her care. Marisol had made arrangements for them both to have a room at the hotel. After the wedding they had planned to head down to the casino in Eagle Pass. Maria and Marla both were going with them. I knew both my mom and aunt would be in good hands.

Our wedding was to start at seven PM with the reception right afterwards. Colin, I had a midnight flight to Hawaii. One of his Air Force buddies owned a chalet on the beach and had graciously offered it to us to use for a week. We would start our honeymoon once we were there. Even though I was not eligible for vacation the firm had given me two weeks off anyway. It was enough time to get ready for the wedding and go on our honeymoon.

Gifts had been coming in for weeks now. Both my apartment and Collins were stacked with packages. We would not open them until after we returned from our honeymoon.

My mom and aunt were planning to stay in San Antonio for a few months, so Colin gave them his apartment to use. He would be moving in with me. The last two days he had spent moving his clothes and personal items to my place. His lease would be up in October and mine in December. By that time, we would decide if we were staying in the apartment or buying a house.

We had already looked at several places. We had not decided yet on where we wanted to buy. We both liked the Dominion area, but I was also partial to the Shavano Park area.

It was time.
Marisol came into my suite with the news. We would have the ceremony followed with pictures. The photographer had already taken dozens of pictures but the ones with Colin and me would be after the ceremony. We had already had pictures taken out at Wyatt's ranch.

I heard the music start. The girls and were ready to go out to the roof area. I stood back and watched as the two little boys stood just at the entrance. I was standing there waiting for my turn to walk when Benji turned and saw me, He blew me a kiss. Then Joshua also blew me a kiss. I blew kisses back after air catching their kisses. Marisol gave them their cue and they walked down the aisle.

Allison and Brittany went next. Both were accompanied by their husbands Benjamin and Joshua. Next Betty went. Marie took both girls to the entrance and at that moment they became scared. They saw all the people sitting and this panicked them, but the twins were right there in no time. They each took a girl by the hand, and all was well.

I then I heard the music change, and I took a moment to collect myself. I prayed a quick prayer and then I walked up to the entrance. Everybody stood up and I glanced around at all the faces. I looked up and saw my kids Allison and Benjamin. They were both smiling big smiles. Allison had tears of happiness on her face. I winked at her as she gave me a thumbs up. I then turned my head to Colin. The look of love on his face mesmerized me.

As I started walking. I kept my eyes on his. When I got closer, he stepped over and took my arm. As we faced the minister, I felt like my life was just beginning. A whole new world was opening for me. I came to Texas to find me and in the process, I found my one true love. My soul mate. The man I would love for the rest of my life.

We repeated our vows and when the minister said you may now kiss your bride Collin took my face in his hands and kissed me. A kiss I felt down to my toes. I heard clapping and yelling, and Colin pulled me closer as he deepened the kiss. Afterwards he whispered in my ear.

"Now for the honeymoon".

Chapter Twenty-Five

After the wedding there were more pictures to take. The wedding party then headed to the reception hall where all the guests were waiting. As soon as Colin and I entered the room everyone stood and clapped. Colin led me to the center of the room and the band started playing. We dance our very first dance as husband and wife. Colin never taking his eyes off my face. I know I glowed with happiness. Anyone watching knew that we were madly in love.

After the song ended the band played an upbeat song and the four littles came out to the dance floor. Collin and I held the hands of the children and all six of us danced. Soon others were joining us on the dance floor. Colin and I took turns dancing with different people, but I always saw his eyes on me. I was dancing with Gary and Colin was dancing with Maria when Colin said to Maria.

"Mind if we switch partners?"

She gladly took Gary's hand and I stepped into Colins and arms. Colin whispered softly in my ear that it was about time he had me back in his arms. I laughed and he kissed me.

Soon the evening started winding down. I spent a little while with the kids kissing and hugging. I picked up each child one by one and told them I loved them, and I would bring them all presents back from Hawaii.

Maria then led me to the dressing room where I slipped out of my wedding dress into a sun dress with matching heels. Maria assured me she would make sure my dress would be well taken care of. She then gathered all my things and I met Colin at the elevator.

He had changed his clothes also. A Porter had already taken our bags to the waiting limo. I turned to my family and blew kisses. As Colin and I stepped into the elevator I tossed my bridal bouquet out the door. I did not know it at the time but later discovered that one of the twins caught it.

We arrived at the airport with thirty minutes to spare. Our flight to Hawaii was leaving at midnight. It was a ten-hour trip with a layover in Los Angeles. We had first class seats, so the flight was comfortable. We tried to sleep but we wound up talking most of the way about the wedding and the reception and what we had planned to do once we were in Hawaii. We had a week to spend doing whatever we wanted.

Colin had made plans for a helicopter trip around the island, and we were both going to try windsurfing. There were shops to visit as well as many historical spots.

One of those spots would be the Arizona where the ship still laid on the ocean floor. Pearl Harbor was a place I had looked forward to the most. Colin of course had already been there as he was once stationed in Hawaii. We would also be attending a luau as well.

I was drifting off to sleep when I suddenly heard that we were about to land .Colin reached for my hand and kissed my fingers.

"Sorry babe you can rest as soon as we reached the hotel."

We would be staying our first night at the Hilton near the airport. We would then rent a Jeep and drive out to Colins friends beach home. Colin had been there lots of times in the past. He said when he was stationed in Hawaii his friend always had beach parties for the enlisted officers. Most had their wives or girlfriends with them but some like Colin were free agents. He had told me he had dated several island women but nothing ever serious. Once most women discovered he was not interested in marriage they soon lost interest in him. I laughed and said what happened when you met me. He said that I had thrown him for so many loops he was dizzy. I laughed and said.

"Dizzy in love? Lucky me."

At that point Colin kissed me until I was dizzy.

We touchdown and Colin and got our bags and a taxi. We headed to the hotel. We checked in at the hotel and a porter took our bags to the eight floor. We stepped off the elevator and the Porter opened our door and set our luggage just inside. Colin tipped him and the Porter left.

Colin picked me up and carried me through the door of the hotel suite. My eyes on his he walked to the middle of the room, and I slowly slid down from his arms. He took my face in his hands and slowly rubbed his lips across mine. I put my arms around him and grabbed his shirt. He continued to slowly tease me. When I moaned, he touched my lips with his tongue, and I grabbed on pulling his tongue into my mouth. We were hungry for each other.

Colin pulled back a glazed look in his eyes. He slowly reached up and pulled the two hairpins holding my hair up. He tossed them on the floor. He ran his fingers through my hair I leaned my head back. He kissed my neck. He ran kisses across my neck to my shoulders. He reached for the zipper of my dress and gently pulled it down. He grabbed my lips and kissed me rubbing his hands up and down my arms. I reached for the buttons on his shirt. I slowly unbutton each button. I pulled his shirt off and tossed it on the floor. I ran my hands up and down his chest I leaned forward and place kisses on his chest up his neck and to his ear. I whispered.

"I want you."

Colin picked me up and carried me to the bed and gently laid me down. He removed my heels. I pulled out his belt unfastening his pants. He stood and dropped them to the floor. I laid back on the pillows and I opened my arms. He came willingly into my embrace. He kissed me and left a trail of kisses down my face to my neck and down further to my chest where he kissed the Crest of my breasts. I arched my back pulled his hair as he continued to rain soft kisses on me. He found the front clasp of my bra and click the snap open. he reached down and pulled my panties down and tossed them behind him. He smiled at me and said.

"You are so beautiful my love."

He ran his fingers down my body. When he touched my stomach, I gasped and arched my body up. His fingers found my throbbing center. He continued to kiss me as he gently massaged me. I moaned over and over. I felt the peaks forming and as hard as I tried not to, I felt the climax coming on. He rubbed harder and I met his fingers with my hips thrusting upward. Colin whispered in my ear.

"Let it go baby" I grabbed his shoulders as wave after wave crashed through me. When I came back to my senses,

I realized he had removed his underwear and I felt his harness as he slowly penetrated me. He wanted slow but I was ready for more. I grabbed onto his manhood with the muscles of my vaginal walls, and he rammed into me. I met him thrust for thrust. I bit into his shoulder as I felt the passion start to grow. Harder and faster, he drove into me. He was holding back his climax until he felt me start to shutter. He then rammed harder into me, and we both climax together. He slowed his thrusting and dropped his body down onto me. I wrapped my legs tightly around him refusing to let him leave my body. I held him tight to me. I ran my nails slowly up and down his back. He laid there until his breathing slowed down. I could feel his heartbeat.

Colin whispered, " Baby I have no words. I love you so much."

" Just kiss me my love."

I slowly released my legs around him he reached over for the top sheet. As he pulled it over us, he laid on his back and pulled me down next to him into his arms. I leaned my face into his neck. I wrapped one arm across his chest and threw my leg over his. He kissed my face and we both closed our eyes and slept.

Epilogue

Two Years Later

Colin and I just celebrated our second anniversary. Being married to him was the greatest joy of my life. More and more every day we had easily settled down to an amazingly comfortable life.

We worked every day. Many weekends were spent out at Wyatt and Betty's ranch.

Colin and I loved riding horses. We even loved working on the ranch. Wyatt and Betty were hard workers and taught us about the everyday running of the ranch.

They also had several programs they offered. We had gone on a lot of weekend camping trips. Riding horses and camping was always a thrill. We met and made a lot of new friends on these excursions.

I found out they also sponsored school programs. They sponsor several in fact. They had a program for children with disabilities. A program for Kinder through fifth grades.

They hosted weekend camp trips for older children in grades six through twelve. I loved helping with those camps.

Last year Betty and I started a summer program for children on the weekends to learn gardening. The children loved taking home vegetables they had a hand in producing.

Colin had been able to cut back on a lot of his trips and after thirty-eight years in the Air Force he was ready to retire.

I was not aware when we married that Colin was extremely wealthy. His parents had left him several insurance policies as well as a huge inheritance. When his brother had been killed in Vietnam Colin was just a young boy. His brother had taken a one-million-dollar insurance policy out and left it to Colin. Colin's parents had invested it wisely and when Colin became an adult, he was worth several million dollars. He had invested wisely.

It was when we were on our honeymoon in Hawaii that he showed me his portfolio. He also had put me as his beneficiary.

Colin said he would never ask me to quit working. He did say if after two years I would agree to retire he would also retire.

Colin wanted to buy a big ranch for us. I was shocked when he said he wanted it to be in Alabama. Colin wanted to raise cows and horses. He also wanted us to be close to the grandchildren.

So, we located a realtor and after several trips to Alabama Collin and Benjamin had found the perfect place. Over 500 acres. The farmhouse was small, so Colin had hired a construction crew to build our dream house.

Colin had several barns built as well. Benjamin had found and hired a half dozen men to work the cattle and horses as they were purchased. Benjamin and Brittany had gone to sales all over the South buying horses and cattle. Wyatt had found a cattle sale in Texas and he and Colin had gone to several auctions.

The house was now built, and I had shopped online for almost everything. Brittney and Alison had mastered minded the decorating. Always sending me pictures and face timing before going ahead with projects.

I wanted a simple one-story farmhouse. The kitchen was huge and sunny with a eat in breakfast nook.

A large dining room with a table large enough to fit twelve people. The den was opened concept to the kitchen. It had a full wall fireplace. Three bedrooms all with en suite bathrooms. The master bedroom opened to the back. The French doors opened to the patio connected to the pool. Two sets of French doors in the den, one on each side of the fireplace also opened to the patio and the pool area. The garage was accessible via the mudroom from the laundry room also adjacent to the kitchen. The house alone was over twenty-five hundred square feet. I told Colin it was a rambling farmhouse. He laughed at my joke but always loved whenever I showed him the decoration ideas.

Colins ranch office was located next to the horse barn. We both would share it. The man Benjamin hired as foreman had moved his family into the original farmhouse. After of course Colin had it remodeled and updated.

Colin had also had a beautiful rock covered bungalow built just for me. It had a porch with Rocking chairs. It had a half bath and a small kitchenette. It was my craft building. It was located directly behind the house across from our bedroom. There were trees and shrubs planted all around. To give the building shade.

I loved this man more and more. He was always thinking of ways to make me smile.

We were scheduled to begin our move within a week. I was so happy to be moving back home. I loved Texas and I was sad about leaving. I also enjoyed my job, but as Colin said my new job was being with him raising horses and cows.

The grand children were getting older, Benjamin and Logan had started school. Sophia and Oliva were already three years old. I was looking forward to spoiling all four grandchildren.

I worked my last day at the law firm. Colin was on his last trip as a Lieutenant Colonel in the United States Air Force. His trip this time was Washington DC where he was honored for all his service. He would be returning later tonight and tomorrow we would be flying to Alabama.

The moving firm would come in and pack all our things and deliver them to our new home. I had spent the day packing our suitcases and making a list for the moving company. Gary and Maria had come by to say goodbye. Maria insisted on coming back to assist with the packing. With the movers under her care, I was secured nothing would be amiss.

it was late when I finally crawled into bed. I knew Colin would be home sometime later tonight. I also know he would wake me when he came to bed. I did not mind. I love being wakened with his kisses and touches. I fell asleep dreaming of Colin.

Bonus Chapter

I went to bed sad, lonely missing Colin so much. Every time I closed my eyes, I could see His Face. This only made me want him more but, after a while I fell asleep.

It must have been a peaceful sleep because I woke feeling on top of the world. As I opened my eyes, I could sense something was different. For one I was on my back which I hardly ever do. And two I felt a heaviness across my stomach. I knew something was up but was afraid to move.

Slowly I turned my head to the right and there beside me was the most beautiful site. I smiled. I just kept looking afraid to move, afraid it would somehow disappear.

As I lay watching I couldn't' believe my eyes. Was this a dream? It did not seem like a dream. It felt so real. I placed my hand on my belly. What I felt was real. My heart was pounding so hard I knew any moment it would wake you.

For it was you, my love. Laying there on your side facing me sleeping so peacefully. Your face was so peaceful. Your hair falling across your forehead. I wanted to touch it, but I dared not. I did not want to wake you. I knew that if you were sleeping you were there. So, I watched you sleep.

Do you know how hard it is to lay by someone you have missed and not touch? After what seemed like forever you stirred. You opened your eyes and smiled at me. With your arm across my belly, you pulled me over to you. I went willingly.

I pushed your hair off your face and put my hands behind your head as I gently pulled your lips to mine. A slow gentle kiss softly touching. We kissed like this for several minutes. You pull me slowly ever closer to you. My arms going around your neck we kiss deeper, harder. As if we were dying of thirst and could not get enough to drink. My hands in your hair. your hands rubbing up and down my back. Your lips move to my neck kissing small pecks all around. Going from one side to the next. I moan and you move to where you are on top of me, and I am laying beneath you.

Your kisses move down my neck to my chest. Your hand lifts my breast, and you gently suck on a nipple. I moan some more and arch my head back. You gather both breast in your hands and take turns going from one to the other. My nipples are so hard and wet, and your breath blows gently on them sending a million shock waves thru me.

You go lower to my belly. With one hand you gently rub a nipple between your fingers.

And the other hand goes lower to my thigh, rubbing up and down. Your sending small kisses across my belly. Your tongue is doing things to me. I close my eyes and arch my back my breathing is so labored.

Your hand on my leg suddenly moves to between my legs. You push my legs apart and your fingers fine the spot that is tinder, a fire that is slowly building inside of me. I moan and with my hand I push your head lower. You kiss me on my leg, moving from one to the other teasing me. I feel your breath blowing against my skin and I can hardly breath.

I know what is coming and I hold my breath as I feel your tongue touching me on my sweet spot. Spasms overtake my body and I moan louder. Your fingers open me wider and you bury your mouth on my womanhood. Your hands move to my hips as you raise them to meet your mouth. Your mouth slowly licks and softly sucks. I feel the passion building in me, but I hold back. I want this to last forever.

Your tongue is busy I know you want me to cum, but I do not. I want to wait for you.

My hands move to your hair, holding your head never wanting this feeling to stop. But I cannot stand it I need to feel you inside me.so I pull your head back and I sit up pulling you to me.

Kissing you I suck your tongue deep into my mouth. I pull you to me tightly my arms around you I fall back on the bed never stopping the kiss. Your hands move up to my head. My hand reaches down to find you hard and throbbing. I spread my legs and guide you into me. My hands on your hips rubbing up to your back.

Slowly you enter me we never stop kissing. I feel you as you fill me. I want you now hard and fast, but you have your own agenda. You push all the way in and just hold it there. I am throbbing so I grip you tightly and you moan. So, you move slow at first but faster and faster.

I feel as if I will explode but I am holding back just letting you move inside me. You start to go faster, your breathing harder. I am holding on to you raising my hips to meet you thrust for thrust.

Finally, we speak our first words .You say, "now baby". I say," yes please yes now".

We rock the bed so hard I wonder if it will stand. As I feel you explode inside me, I am thrown into ecstasy. We cum together and it last forever. Even after its over you do not stop, just rocking me softly.

Finally, you stop, and you give me the sweetest kiss, and smiling at me you say, "good morning darling, Lets go home to Alabama."

The End

I hope you enjoyed Maggie's and Colin's love story. Be sure to watch for Harper's and Alejandro's Love story in **Love in New Mexico.**

Coming soon

Made in the USA
Columbia, SC
18 August 2023